Plea
Books

www\

SPECIAL MESSAGE TO READERS

THE ULVERSCROFT FOUNDATION
(registered UK charity number 264873)

was established in 1972 to provide funds for research, diagnosis and treatment of eye diseases.
Examples of major projects funded by the Ulverscroft Foundation are:-

- The Children's Eye Unit at Moorfields Eye Hospital, London
- The Ulverscroft Children's Eye Unit at Great Ormond Street Hospital for Sick Children
- Funding research into eye diseases and treatment at the Department of Ophthalmology, University of Leicester
- The Ulverscroft Vision Research Group, Institute of Child Health
- Twin operating theatres at the Western Ophthalmic Hospital, London
- The Chair of Ophthalmology at the Royal Australian College of Ophthalmologists

You can help further the work of the Foundation by making a donation or leaving a legacy.
Every contribution is gratefully received. If you would like to help support the Foundation or require further information, please contact:

THE ULVERSCROFT FOUNDATION
The Green, Bradgate Road, Anstey
Leicester LE7 7FU, England
Tel: (0116) 236 4325

website: www.foundation.ulverscroft.com

BLUEPRINT FOR DESTRUCTION

At the height of the Cold War, British Secret Service Agent Steve Carradine faces his most dangerous assignment to date. His investigations begin in London, before moving to America. Here Carradine follows a trail of dead bodies as he seeks to penetrate to the heart of a vast organisation known as the Red Dragon. Carradine traces their agents to Station K, an underground city buried far beneath the Arctic ice, powered by an atomic reactor. And it is here that Carradine uncovers the Red Dragon's blueprint for destruction . . .

MANNING K. ROBERTSON

BLUEPRINT FOR DESTRUCTION

Complete and Unabridged

LINFORD
Leicester

First published in Great Britain

First Linford Edition
published 2014

A catalogue record for this book is available
from the British Library.

ISBN 978–1–4448–2050–8

Published by
F. A. Thorpe (Publishing)
Anstey, Leicestershire

Set by Words & Graphics Ltd.
Anstey, Leicestershire
Printed and bound in Great Britain by
T. J. International Ltd., Padstow, Cornwall

This book is printed on acid-free paper

1

Checkout

The fifty-mile stretch of white concrete highway that ran as straight as a die through the New Mexico desert, now gleaming with a faint sheen in the deep purple of the starlit evening, had not been there when Minden had last been to this part of America. Now it seemed an integral part of the scene, reminding him all too vividly of the speed with which these Americans worked when they had some definite goal in view.

Minden was not usually a reflective man. Inwardly, he knew that unless he succeeded in this particular mission he would not only be written off by his superiors, but they would take steps to see that he did not live to endanger any other agents working for them in this country. This was one of the inescapable facts of life with which he had been forced to live for almost twenty years, a sword of Damocles hanging internally over his head on a very slender thread indeed. Somehow, he had lasted longer than most; for the man who directed these operations had a patience which tended to wear thin with the passing years and whenever he looked back on his life objectively he was forced to admit to himself that he had done little of real value, nothing dramatic.

Twenty years ago, when the end of the war had divided Germany into two separate states, he could have taken the other path — a job in one of the factories in East Berlin; but after nine years in the SS he was not made that way. A short, broad-shouldered man, his iron-grey hair still curling a little around the temples, short-cropped over the rest of his head, he continued to live by the only moral code which Intelligence workers knew — that the results they obtained were their only justification for existence. The results that he had obtained over the past ten years had been sufficient to keep him in his present position: a mediocre figure, tolerated perhaps — but for how long? It seemed odd how long it had taken him to realise, fully, that for him the writing was on the wall.

Cornish, seated behind the wheel of the Pontiac, eased himself into a more upright position. His cream tussore suit, almost white, gleamed incongruously in the shadowed interior of the car. He stared through the windscreen of the car along a deserted stretch of the highway. Then he glanced down at the luminous watch on his wrist.

'If he's on time — and he usually is — we have another twenty minutes to wait,' said Cornish.

'You are getting impatient, perhaps?' It was more of a statement than a question, but Cornish shook his head almost instinctively. 'No, but it's a little difficult to be completely calm at a time like this. You know, of course, that they have their checkpoints all the way along the highway. If he is so much as two minutes late at any point they send out a car to find out why.'

Minden lit a cigarette. Blowing smoke

through his pursed lips, he stared sightlessly into the deep purple darkness beyond the windscreen. 'How can you be so sure he will have the information with him?'

Cornish's faint laugh was indulgent. 'My friend, you forget that I have access to the records of every man who works in the Establishment.'

Minden nodded, satisfied. He knew a little more about Cornish than the other supposed; he had seen his dossier, which contained the photograph just inside the blue and white cover — a photograph that had been taken the previous year, although it was extremely doubtful if Cornish knew it had been taken. Cornish occupied a special position in the Organisation. His usefulness rested on the fact that he did, as he had just said, have access to top-secret documents relating to every man who worked for the American government on this particular defence project. Until 1939 he had been a minor clerk in one of the Boeing Aircraft Establishments, but during the war he had been seconded to the Manhattan Project, still in a minor role.

Then, with the end of the war, there had been vast, far-reaching changes in the set-up of the American Defence Department, particularly in those sectors dealing with the siting of atomic weapons to be used in defence of the country in the event of a global war. Several of the top-ranking scientists had resigned their posts. It had not been difficult for Minden to discover why they had chosen to do this. While America was at war, patriotism coupled with the strict laws in force during wartime had prevailed on these men to continue, unabated, their work on nuclear weapons. With the final defeat of Japan and his own country, these restrictions no longer held and men who could, more than anyone else, realise the full and terrible destructive power of the weapons they had developed, refused to carry out work on them any longer. Perhaps they had the vision to see the direction in which the politicians would lead them; perhaps they foresaw the dread consequences of what they had done so willingly in time of crisis. Whatever the reason, they refused to continue their work and the new style began. With the inevitable shake-up, minor officials suddenly assumed a greater importance. Naturally, the FBI checked on each of these men; but here and there, they passed over those whose allegiance was elsewhere than to the United States. Such a man was Albert Cornish.

Bending down, Cornish opened the glove compartment and took out a thermos flask and a couple of paper cups. 'You want some coffee?' he said. 'Take some of the chill out of your bones.'

'Very well.' He accepted the cup that the other held out to him, sat back in the seat and sipped the hot coffee, contentedly. There was one thing to be said for the Americans, he thought; they certainly knew how to make coffee.

'Will it be absolutely necessary to kill him?' Cornish's voice was flat.

'Of course. Perhaps you have forgotten the way in which the Organisation works. Or is it that this is the first time you have seen this side of our work?' Minden spoke in a slightly puzzled intonation.

'I haven't forgotten.' Cornish drained

his coffee, crumpled up the paper cup and tossed it out through the half-open window. He deliberately wiped the back of his hand across his mouth, then reached into the rear seat and pulled out the leather case containing the high-powered binoculars. 'It's merely that it seems such an unnecessary complication.'

'And your mind is always so very tidy,' said the other sarcastically. He screwed up his own cup, placed it carefully back in the glove compartment and took out the long-barrelled pistol which lay there. Screwing the silencer attachment onto the end of the barrel, he gave a satisfied nod and turned to the other. 'See anything yet? He should be in sight by now.'

'Nothing,' murmured Cornish. He adjusted the focusing screw of the binoculars with the tips of his fingers as he spoke. A moment later, he gave a faint sigh. 'Yes, there he is!' He lowered the binoculars and handed them to Minden. 'Care to take a look?'

'*Danke.*' Minden rested his elbows on the dashboard, holding the binoculars rigid, pressing them into his eyes. He focused them on the point where the grey-white strip of the highway faded abruptly into the general, overall darkness of the desert. He could just make out the faint division between sky and earth and then, faint but unmistakable, the twin head-lights of an approaching car. He guessed that it was perhaps five or six miles away. 'Can you be sure that it's him?'

Patiently, Cornish said: 'I've checked his timing and route for the past three weeks. Always, he has been on time, whether he's carrying documents or not.'

'And he's alone?'

'Yes. I'm certain of it.'

'Good. Then you know what to do. If the idea of killing him does not appeal to you, leave that part to me.'

Without answering, Cornish turned the ignition key and depressed the accelerator pedal gently, the powerful engine purring softly with a suppressed song of power beneath the long bonnet. He eased the gear lever into position and sat tensed with the clutch still depressed, ready to move as soon as the other gave the order. Out of the corner of his eye, he watched

Minden, leaning forward with the binoculars still thrust tightly against his eyes. The other did not move as much as a muscle as he watched the headlights creep nearer along the arrow-straight highway. Poised like that, he reminded Cornish of a tiger he had once seen: crouched, ready to spring, to crush and destroy. His first impression of Carl Minden had been one of surprise, for there had not been that air of ruthless determination about this man that he had been expecting from what he had heard of him from other sources; at least, it had not been apparent then. Now he realised that it had been there all the time, but had been merely dormant, waiting for the moment when it should surge up to the surface and wipe his body clean of all other emotions.

'All right?' he asked finally, his voice a harsh whisper.

'Switch on the headlights when I tell you,' said Minden out of the corner of his mouth, 'and then move across the highway to block the other side of the road.'

'Suppose that he doesn't stop?' Doubts seized the other at this last moment.

'Then it will mean the end of us and you'll be past caring about what the Organisation will do to you as the price of failure.'

There was a slow, soft rumble in the distance. The twin headlights of the oncoming car were clearly visible now, even without the enhanced vision of the binoculars, and Minden tossed them quickly into the back seat as he straightened up and said harshly: 'Now!'

There was a soft click as Cornish switched on the headlights. The twin beams lanced out with a surprising suddenness, spearing through the darkness ahead of them. A moment later, he let in the clutch and spun the wheel, moving the car directly across the highway in front of the other vehicle. Minden tensed himself in his seat and fought down the faint germ of panic that churned deep within him.

They teach you how to kill and how to defend yourself against another attack armed with a gun, a knife, or any other weapon. They teach you that the chances of survival are so stacked against the man in this dangerous game that one must

10

face the possibility of death with equanimity. Yet in spite of all this careful coaching and preparation, the sight of headlights glaring and flashing their warning of impending disaster, and the high-pitched scream of brakes and tortured rubber, could still tie his stomach into knots and make him temporarily forget everything in the surging, abysmal terror of self-preservation.

Dipping and rising hypnotically, swinging from side to side as the driver of the other car fought to bring it under control, the brilliant, all-pervading glare of the powerful lights threatened to blind him as he felt Cornish stamp down on the brakes, bringing the Pontiac to a lurching halt, slewed at an angle across the northbound section of the highway.

Had they left it too late? For one terrifying moment, he felt certain they had overplayed their hand, cut things just a little too fine.

Now he could hear the rasping whine of the six cylinders. The high-pitched whine changed abruptly to a shattering roar that bit deeply at his overstretched nerves. Minden got a glimpse of the other car swerving violently as it careened off the edge of the highway, past the front of the Pontiac's bonnet, glancing along the rough concrete of the verge and then going like hell over the stretch of rough ground that lay beyond, ploughing through a dozen stunted bushes before it came to a halt, headlights staring crazily into the darkness of the night sky.

Gripping the silenced pistol, Minden opened the door, climbed out and ran swiftly towards the other car. Minutes — seconds — were precious now. It was impossible to tell if the driver was alive, even conscious. Miraculously, except for splintered glass in one of the headlights and a twisted bumper, the other car seemed to be undamaged. Wrenching open the door, he peered inside. The driver was there, slumped over the wheel, his face turned away from Minden. A slim black briefcase was on the seat beside him.

There was, as usual, a faint light from the courtesy lamp set in the roof of the car just above the dashboard. Reaching out, Minden grabbed the briefcase, drew it along the seat, and almost had it when the man lying behind the wheel suddenly moved. The sweat was beading on Minden's face as he saw the other turn his head, eyes wide open, looking up into his. There was a smear of blood on the other's cheek and a gash just above the left eye, but the man appeared to be fully conscious; he seemed to have been faking unconsciousness, waiting for Minden to make the first move.

For a moment, the other's move took Minden completely by surprise. Then in the faint light he saw the glint of metal in the other's hand, and caught a glimpse of the snub-nosed automatic. Minden's muscles coiled like those of a snake. There was no room now inside the car to line up the gun on the other's body, to be absolutely sure of hitting a vital spot with a single shot. His right hand flickered as he thrust forward with the gun. In one violent corkscrew of motion, he twisted himself sharply around, the barrel catching the other on the side of the head just behind the ear.

Minden had planned for the other's

savage reflex action. He stepped back a pace as the other jerked up the automatic, squeezed off a single shot, felt the wind of the slug pass his face, and heard it hit the door of the car and ricochet into the darkness. The hard blow had dazed the other and before he could fully recover, Minden slammed the barrel down again — this time with all of the strength in his body behind the wicked, downwards swing. The other uttered a muffled moan. With a slither and a crack of the head against the dashboard the other slid sideways, falling off the front seat, arms and legs dangling onto the floor.

For a moment Minden crouched there, breathing hard. He stared at the limp body of the man in front of him, at the dark stain on the side of his head. Then, automatically, he reached out and felt the wrist. There was no detectable pulse beating in the vein. Letting the limp arm fall onto the seat, he backed out of the car, picked up the briefcase and sprinted over to the Pontiac. Cornish's grey face stared out at him as he opened the door and got inside.

'Did you get the briefcase?' he asked anxiously.

'It's here,' muttered Minden. 'Now get out of here.' He slammed the door of the car shut behind him as Cornish let in the clutch. The warm-heated engine murmured softly as they began to move, gathering speed. Minden twisted in his seat and peered through the window behind them, looking back along the highway. He could just make out the shape of the wrecked car, the probing beams of the twin headlights lancing up into the starlit heavens at a ludicrous angle.

It would be ten minutes yet before that car was supposed to pass through the checkpoint ten miles further along the road; but in spite of this, every minute — every second — was a bonus. Now that the worst was over, Cornish was going like hell. There was no traffic on the road at this time of night and Cornish kept up a good speed along the straight highway for five miles before pulling off at a sharp command from the man seated beside him. Springs creaked in protest while the wheel jerked like a live thing under Cornish's hands. Then they were on a dirt track leading off towards the distant hills, the headlights picking out the rough, uneven surface, rising and falling as they bounced and jolted over a stretch of the roughest terrain that Minden had known. He let out his breath in a quiet hiss. Wiping his sweating hands on his trousers, he sat back in the seat, still clutching the precious briefcase between his hands.

* * *

There was a brilliant red light gleaming above the door at the end of the corridor as Steve Carradine stepped out of the lift and made his way down the quiet passage with the four closed doors, two at either side. He pressed the switch on the side of the door and waited for a moment until the light flicked to green, then back to red, before opening the door and stepping inside. Closing the door softly behind him, he glanced across to the man seated behind the desk. There was nothing outwardly startling in the other's appearance. His cherubic countenance glistened a little in the hot sunlight, which streamed through the window behind him. He was writing on the pad in front of him as Carradine entered, but pushed it away and gestured to the chair immediately opposite him. Carradine sat down, thrust his legs out straight in front of him and waited for the other to speak.

'I've asked the Chief of Staff to come along and join us,' he said evenly. He looked carefully at Carradine. 'Do you find it too hot?' Then without waiting for a reply, pressed the button on the desk and a hidden fan began to whir softly in the ceiling, adding its faint background hum to the distant sound of the London traffic far below.

There was something coming, Carradine thought wearily. He settled himself more comfortably in his chair. For the past three months, during one of the hottest summers he had ever known in London, he had merely idled his way around Headquarters, doing little of interest, simply because it had been the stated policy that every agent was to do his share of the routine work of the Section. Many times, he found himself wishing that some trouble would break out somewhere in the world, giving him the chance to get away from the humdrum affairs here in London.

A sharp, peremptory buzz jerked his thoughts back to the present. The other touched another button and a moment later, the door opened and Forbes, the Chief of Staff, came in. He nodded to Carradine, walked over and seated himself on the other chair.

'Now we'll get down to business,' the Chief said. Glancing at Carradine, he added seriously: 'Tell me, are you tired of sitting around here while your colleagues are having the time of their lives all over the globe? I understand what it's like for someone of your temperament. If you are, then I think we may have an assignment for you which you'll like.'

Carradine raised his brows a little. 'Indeed, sir.'

'Yes. Though what I have in mind is, I'm afraid, a little out of the ordinary, even for us.'

Carradine sat back in his chair. He had

thought that by now, he was used to any surprises that the other might spring on him; but he had the feeling ever since the call had come through to his office for him to go up to see the Chief, that this was something a little different from anything he had done before. 'I must confess that I had already guessed that much, sir.'

'Good. Then I'll leave Forbes here to tell you as much as we know already. It isn't much, but it will give you an idea of what has been asked of us.'

Forbes cleared his throat, then began: 'Briefly, this is what happened. You know that the Americans have set up several defensive posts around the country, as well as having some abroad, both here, in Europe and along the Red frontier with Turkey. The whereabouts of some of these are well known in certain circles; they've been there for so long now that everybody knows of their existence. The Americans don't mind, really. It takes people's eyes off the real thing, the secret bases they don't want anybody to know a thing about.'

19

Carradine leaned forward a little, interested. 'But now somebody does know something about them and the Yanks are worried. Is that it?'

Forbes hesitated, then he shrugged. 'Exactly. Naturally, they are extremely worried.'

'I can understand that. But what does it have to do with us?'

'Strictly speaking — nothing. Normally, we would keep out of it. They have, however, now asked for our help.'

Carradine looked suitably surprised. From the edge of his vision, he noticed the faint glitter in the Chief's eyes. 'Why should they do that? They have their own men in this field.'

Forbes nodded. 'That is quite true,' he said in his faintly pompous tone. 'Unfortunately, they have already lost three of their best men and it's beginning to look as though their agents are too well-known to be of any real value in this particular task.'

'Then I take it that there is a very well-organised group working in America, far better than anything they've come across before.'

Forbes was about to speak when the Chief interjected. 'This Organisation must have been in existence for several years to build up such a network of good men throughout the country. It's all the more surprising that the FBI have heard nothing of them until a few months ago. Evidently they've been prepared for one purpose only — to get this vital secret information as quickly and efficiently as possible. The way they have been working so far indicates that unless they're stopped very soon, they will be completely successful.'

'Is there any lead to go on? Do we know the identity of any of these agents?'

'Unfortunately — no.'

'I see.' Carradine shrugged his shoulders. That presented some difficulties.

'I wonder if you do,' the Chief went on. 'Usually, with a job like this, we know at least one of their men. I suppose that if the Russians were behind this, the same might apply. Americans are quite good at keeping an eye on anyone they suspect even slightly in their country, big as it is.'

Carradine felt his fingers grip the sides

of the chair a little more tightly, although he gave no other outward sign of his surprise. 'Then we can take it that the Reds are not at the back of it, sir?' he inquired politely.

'Oh, sorry, my boy. Didn't I mention it?' There was a faintly apologetic note to the other's voice. 'We're pretty certain — not one hundred percent, but near enough as makes no difference — that the Red Chinese are at the back of this.'

'Oh Lord,' muttered Carradine fervently.

'Exactly. We may even need His help before we're through with this one.'

Carradine sighed. The way the other said it, it sounded almost like a prayer; and in all of his career, and his dealings with the Chief, he had never known the other talk like this.

'Does it make you feel apprehensive?'

'A little, sir,' Carradine replied.

'Fine.' The other beamed at him. 'I always believe that a man who says he's neither apprehensive nor afraid when facing an assignment such as this, is either a liar or a fool, and I have no time for either.' He looked at Carradine thoughtfully for a long moment, then observed: 'I think you'll do. You have had a reasonable spell behind the desk. If I keep you there too long you'll become rusty and of no further use to me.' A pause, then: 'I take it you're willing to take the job?'

'Of course, sir.'

'Excellent.' He knew, inwardly, that he could not have chosen a better man. Carradine's file was known intimately to him, as were those of every other agent under his command. Everyone had been hand-picked and intensively trained. Their work was not always the exciting, romantic life that people outside tended to believe it to be. Danger and death were their constant elbow companions. Each time a man went out on a mission, he wondered himself whether he would ever see that man alive again, or whether the agent would simply vanish from the face of the earth, never to be seen or heard of again.

It was a risk these men took willingly. This was their life, and so very often it turned out to be a dirty, evil thing. One had to fight evil and tyranny with similar weapons, and quite often it involved innocent people doing disagreeable things that any self-respecting man would normally shun completely.

'When do I leave, sir?'

The chief glanced sideways at Forbes, then looked back. 'Arrangements will be made for you to fly out to New York in four days' time. During the intervening period, I want you to learn everything you can and be sure that you are back up to scratch again. These few months of soft living may have changed you. I don't want to leave anything to chance.' A broad grin appeared briefly on his fleshy features. 'After all, you will have to be on your mettle to prove that we are just as good, if not better, than our counterparts in the FBI.'

'Upon arrival in New York,' said Forbes quietly, 'you will contact a man named Dean. This is his address — the only place where you will make contact with him. You understand?'

'Perfectly,' said Carradine as Forbes

24

wrote the name and address on a slip of paper and handed it to him.

'There is a possibility that this enemy organisation which is operating inside America knows of Dean's existence; and more important still, that he is to be your contact.' Forbes looked sad at the prospect — almost, thought Carradine with an inward smile, as if he were really worried about him. He was not surprised at Forbes' insistence on the secrecy. Security was one thing that this man lived for. He thought security; dreamed it. He doubted if the Chief was more security-conscious. Well, maybe it was just as well that they had a man like Forbes here. Sometimes it was necessary to curb the natural exuberance of the agents who received their orders from here and went out into various countries to pit their wits against those who plotted against the peace and security of the world.

'Since I shall be operating virtually on my own, except for Dean, can you tell me anything of the size of this organisation I shall be fighting?'

'Huge,' said Forbes quietly. 'We know

so very little about it that I doubt if anyone in the Western world can give anything but a very vague estimate. But there is no doubt that it has succeeded in spreading its tentacles into every major city in the States.' He shrugged his shoulders uneasily. 'For all we know, there may be an odd tentacle or two in this country.'

'I'm sure that if there were, you would have been the first to hear of it,' put in the Chief calmly. 'But we seem to be straying a little from the point.' His eyes took on their hard, calculating, foxy look. 'Frankly, I was not quite sure that it would be a good thing, as far as we were concerned, to have one of our agents working like this for the Americans. I think the PM was of the same mind, but there are other factors operating here which need not concern you and it was these, more than anything else, which decided things.'

'I think I've got the full picture now, sir,' Carradine said softly.

'Good. Remember what I said earlier. See that you're back in form after your desk job. It's surprising how soon a man's reflexes slow to danger point. I know that you're too good a man to leave anything to chance.' He got to his feet. 'In the meantime, I'll have all the necessary arrangements made.' He paused, then said gently, as if a sudden thought had just struck him: 'There is one man who may be able to help you before you leave. I suggest that you go along and have a word with him. His name is Sen Yi. He owns a small restaurant in one of the backwaters of London. Not a very prepossessing place from all accounts, but it seems that he fought with the communists against Chiang Kai-Shek and was one of their top officials until he discovered he could no longer stomach some of the things they were doing in the name of communism. He managed to slip over the frontier into Hong Kong a couple of years ago, stayed there for eighteen months and then came to England. Apparently he is quite willing to tell as much as he can about the Red Dragon.'

'That's the name of the organisation in America, sir?' asked Carradine.

The other leaned forward and placed

his knuckled hands on the desk in front of him. 'The Red Dragon is the organisation as it exists inside Communist China today. That which is operating inside America is merely an offshoot of it, but no less dangerous, I'm sure.'

Carradine's answering smile was taut and he felt his mind sharpen; quite suddenly, the faint rumble of the distant London traffic down below seemed to be enhanced and curiously magnified, as if he were able to pick out every tiny sound more clearly. This was the first time in his career that he had bumped up against the Chinese and he had the funny feeling that they would prove to be more dangerous and more difficult to assess than any of the other enemies he had met in the past. It was a little surprising, though, that he had not come up against them earlier. Since they had exploded their own atomic bomb — or some weapon in that class, since details were naturally extremely vague — he had been expecting them to move in on the Western capitals, hoping to gain as much information as they could of the defence systems of America and Europe. There had been a curious slackening of the tension between the Russians and the West. Was this to be the prelude to the new menace?

He sat back, waiting patiently to see if there was anything more. The Chief straightened up.

'Well, I think that's all I have for you now, Carradine. You'll check with Sen Yi as soon as possible.'

'Can we be entirely sure that he can be trusted, sir?' Carradine asked pointedly as he pushed back his chair and got to his feet.

Forbes said tautly: 'Naturally, we cannot be one hundred percent certain. He may be a double agent, still working for the Communists. He is, however, the only lead we have at present, unless the Americans have succeeded in coming up with something fresh within the last week or so. Watch your step with him and if there are any facts he gives you, which we can verify from other sources, then check on them too. We have had him under close surveillance since he arrived here and he was also watched pretty closely while in Hong Kong.' He twitched his lips into a thin smile, but his face retained its sombre expression. 'Naturally we are all aware of the chief characteristic of the Chinese — their infinite patience and inscrutability. At the moment, we must simply play them at their own game.'

One of the prerequisites of a good agent was the ability to distinguish between a genuine informant and a double agent. Caaradine recalled that they had lost some good men because of failure to do this. So far, he had been lucky. But there was always the nagging fear in the back of the mind that luck could be a very fickle goddess.

As he left the room and made his way slowly through the various corridors inside the building, he found himself reflecting more than usual on life and death. It was part of his life, as well as that of his colleagues, to kill. Sometimes it was inevitable; sometimes it was necessary only to make things easier for himself and to ensure his own safety. He had never liked it, although there had been men who deserved to die — men who were undeniably evil. Yet with most of them, even telling himself that one man had died so that thousands more might live did not help to salve his conscience. Perhaps, he thought wearily, as he went out into the bustling streets, that was his one big weakness. He still had a conscience that pricked him now and again.

2

The Red Dragon

It was five o'clock that same afternoon when Carradine turned the corner of the narrow road that led him down into a part of London with which he was only vaguely familiar. It was strange to reflect that he was less than a quarter of a mile from the end of the Strand with its bright lights, its theatres and glittering neon signs. Here was a world of cool dimness, the lights muted, as if reticent to be seen. Carradine was suddenly tense, peering about him. He was halfway along the narrow, winding street before he noticed the pale blue sign over a doorway that was set below the level of the street.

Making his way slowly and quietly down the stone steps, he paused in front of the door, then pushed it open and went inside. A bell chimed softly in the distance somewhere. A short Chinese appeared as if by magic from nowhere.

Without a word, the other led the way into the dimly-lit interior, through the tables and to a small alcove set in the far wall. Setting the menu in front of him, he stepped back and waited.

Carradine scanned the menu, gave his order, handed the card back to the waiter, then said in a quiet tone: 'Is Sen Yi available?'

For a moment, the waiter gave him a nervous scrutiny then nodded, brushed aside the rattling bamboo curtain and disappeared from sight. Carradine sat back and let his gaze wander around the small restaurant. There were few other customers. A couple of rough-looking characters were seated near the low bar at the far end of the room. They had their heads turned up, watching him intently, but they lowered their eyes and looked away when they saw he had noticed them and was looking in their direction. The others were Chinese from this quarter of London. Like the Indians and Jamaicans, they tended to form themselves into tight little communities, mixing with the population during

the daytime but at night keeping themselves much to themselves.

The waiter came back, set the steaming
dish of fried chicken and bamboo shoots
in front of him, brought a rice wine and
then moved away before Carradine could
say anything. Shrugging resignedly, he
bent over the food and began to eat slowly.
It was delicious, cooked as only the
Chinese knew how.

He was halfway through it when he
became aware that the bamboo curtain
had been pushed apart and a man was
standing there watching him. How long
the other had been there, he did not
know. Glancing up swiftly, he stared into
the seamed face of Sen Yi. The other was
of indeterminate age and could have been
anything from forty-five to seventy, he
guessed.

'I understand that you wish to speak
with me,' said the other, his tone calm
and polite.

'You are Sen Yi?' Carradine said. It was
more of a statement than a question.

The other gave a grave nod. 'That is my
name.'

'Won't you sit down?' Carradine waved a hand towards the other chair. 'I've been told that you may be able to give me some vital information.'

For a second, the other's mask of inscrutability vanished. Then he moved around the table and sat down, regarding Carradine with the utmost gravity.

'In what way can I help you?'

Lowering his voice, Carradine said: 'Can we be overheard from here?'

'No.' Sen Yi gave a slight shake of his head. 'It is quite safe.'

'Good.' Carradine came straight to the point. 'I want you to tell me about the Red Dragon.'

The other's eyes narrowed down to mere slits. 'The Red Dragon,' he said sibilantly, without the slightest trace of inflection.

Carradine smiled faintly. 'I know quite a lot about you, Sen Yi. About your work in China before you fled to Hong Kong. My informant was quite certain that you could help me.'

'To my humble perception, it would appear that you are a member of the

35

British Security Service. Am I not correct?'

'Perhaps it might be that the less you know of this matter, the better,' Carradine said.

Sen Yi locked his gaze with Carradine's. 'What is it that you wish to know of the Red Dragon?'

'As much as you can tell me, particularly of that branch which is operating in the West.'

'There are many secret societies in China — and the Red Dragon is the most deadly and dangerous. The Ruling Party uses it mainly to keep the mass of the people under their control, just as the Nazi Party created and used their Gestapo. They took some of the methods used by both the Gestapo and the Kempetai in Japan, and modified them to suit their own temperament.'

'And you actually worked for them before you left China?' Carradine queried.

'For eight years,' Sen Yi murmured softly. 'But you must understand, my friend, that even inside the Red Dragon organisation, there are a multitude of tiny, airtight compartments, each having its own purpose, its own mission to fulfil. Those who work in one section know little, if anything, of the work of others.'

'I see.' This was what Carradine had half-suspected. It meant that Sen Yi could probably tell him very little of the American offshoot of the organisation, even if he was willing to do so. 'What can you tell me then?'

'Very little. They are mainly a counter-espionage organisation, but I suspect that the group inside America exists for little more than spying on the American defence sites.'

'That much we already know. Can you give me any names?'

'There is a man called Minden. If he is still alive, he could be working for them.'

'A German?' Carradine looked surprised.

'From East Germany,' corrected the other. 'I understand that he was with the Gestapo since its inception. When the war ended in Europe, he was forced to go underground, otherwise he would have suffered the same fate as other Nazis did. He was in Russia for two years and then went to China. He brought several secret documents with him, some from Russia. This was at the time when the rift between China and Russia was just beginning to widen a little. He could not have taken anything more valuable. It was this which made them accept him, more than anything else.'

'He sounds like a dangerous and unscrupulous man. How could the Red Dragon be so certain that he would not do the same thing again, taking some of *their* secrets with him?'

'Naturally,' the other spread his hands a little on top of the table, 'that is a possibility — but no more than that. The tentacles of the Red Dragon are spread throughout the world in every major city. But it does not advertise its presence as many others do. I think that Minden knows, only too well, that there is nowhere — nowhere at all — in the whole world where he is beyond the reach of them.'

'And does that not also apply to you?'

'Of course.' Sen Yi bowed his head slightly. 'By telling you even this, I shall have placed a noose around my neck or a knife in my back.'

Carradine stared at the little man who sat opposite him; at the quiet, almost serene features. It was difficult, if not impossible, for him to believe that Sen Yi meant what he said, when he claimed he had already pronounced his own death sentence. In the past he had met men from the other side of the Iron Curtain, men whose mission had been to destroy him, men who had failed in that mission and been ordered back to Russia. It required no stretch of the imagination to visualise what their reception would be once they arrived back in the Soviet Union. A professional spy was allowed one mistake as far as Section M was concerned. With the Russians, he was not even allowed that. But that was the first time he had ever sat with a man and heard him discuss his own death so quietly and calmly.

Sen Yi must have learned many State secrets during the time he worked with the Red Dragon organisation inside Communist China; and even at that time, he must have known that one day, this knowledge might have extremely dangerous consequences for him. Sitting in that quiet room, Carradine felt a little of the terror that must have come to this man in those days several years before and wondered if that terror had grown with the passage of time. He himself has said that even here in London, he was not safe from these men. In spite of himself, he glanced out of the corner of his eye at the other customers in the small restaurant and found his gaze fixed on the two men on the other side of the room. They were now talking together in low voices, occasionally looking almost furtively over their shoulders towards the dimly-lit alcove.

Any one of the people in the restaurant could be an agent of the Red Dragon, watching Sen Yi and any of his acquaintances. There was, perhaps, no front in the world in which the agents of Red China were not quietly and stealthily advancing, content to allow the West to concentrate all of its attentions on the Soviet agents whose tactics, although discrete and following a carefully conceived and planned policy, were blundering when compared with those of the Chinese. Perhaps it was something to do with the way the Oriental mind worked, he reflected as he sipped the small cup of subtly scented tea.

'There is nothing more you can tell me?' Every tiny grain of information he could get from the other might be instrumental in saving his life.

'Nothing, but — ' Sen Yi hesitated, threw a quick glance about him, then rose smoothly to his feet, scarcely moving the chair on which he had been sitting. Bending forward slowly, he said in a sibilant whisper, 'It may be dangerous for you to remain here. There are too many eyes and ears even in this part of London. You are used to danger, I can tell; but with the Red Dragon, it can strike without warning and from unexpected directions.'

Carradine tensed. The other stared down at him for a long moment, then moved around the table and vanished

41

through the curtain. Carradine shook himself. What the hell had all this been about? A German named Minden working in America on behalf of the Communist Chinese? Was there a chance that Sen Yi had told him all of this for a reason other than to help him? He had guessed from the very beginning that he was working for the British Secret Service. It was also likely that *he* was still working for the Red Dragon and all the information he had just given him had been false.

He finished the tea, motioned to the waiter and paid his bill. Outside, the sun was getting lower and in the long shadows thrown across the narrow alley, he could feel the distinct chill that had somehow lain hidden under the heat of the day. There were few people in sight, although the faint hum of the traffic in the main street was audible above the screaming, high-pitched cries of the children from the tenements on either side. Carradine walked slowly and watched the shadows around him. There was an odd stillness all about him now, one which he had felt on several previous occasions. He was waiting for something — he was not sure what — to happen. He only knew that this feeling had not been there when he had walked down this narrow alley towards the restaurant.

Halfway along the alley, he paused and turned his head slowly, apparently incuriously, looking back in the direction of the restaurant. He had the strong sensation that those two rough-looking characters he had seen there would be following him, keeping well in the shadows.

But Carradine was mistaken. There was no one there. He could just see the door of the restaurant. It was closed and in the faint light, the windows on either side of it glistened dully. He shrugged. So he had been wrong. He felt a little let down. It was not usual for his sixth sense to betray him like this.

His pace had slowed a fraction as he turned to survey the alley behind him. Now he lengthened his stride a little, still not relaxed. A couple of Chinese children, their faces curiously expressionless in the gloom, ran chattering shrilly from the house on his left, raced across the alley and vanished into the dimness of one of the buildings on the other side. A sudden stillness settled on the place. He felt a prickle of sweat break out on his forehead. He strained his eyes into the long shadows.

He was still expecting trouble and consequently, he was ready for it when it materialised abruptly. As the dim shape launched itself from the narrow opening, he was completely on balance, right arm coming up instinctively. There was a faint gleam of light reflected from the long, curved blade of the knife in his assailant's hand. His forearm smashed savagely against the other as the man swung downward. The blow threw the other's knife arm off-target, staggering him against the wall. But he still retained his tight-fisted grip on the knife, lips drawn back in a savage snarl, eyes narrowed down to mere slits.

Carradine felt a sense of surprise. This was not one of the two men he had seen in the restaurant. He had never seen this man before yet there was no doubting the other's intention of killing him. He had no chance to go for the gun in its holster beneath his left arm. Already, the other had recovered and was moving in again.

Pivoting his body from the waist, Carradine waited. The other was breathing quickly and heavily, his chest heaving. In the loose-fitting coat and trousers, his body seemed oddly shapeless. The knife descending in a glittering arc was less than six inches from Carradine's throat when he sidestepped swiftly, straightened his fingers and jabbed them with a savage force into the pit of the other's exposed body. Fingers spread a little for rigidity, he used just enough force to paralyse the other's stomach muscles. A little more force behind the blow would have killed the man instantly. As it was, the man reeled back against the wall, the knife dropping from his nerveless fingers, a gasp of agony bleating from between his lips. His face screwed up into a grimace of agony as Carradine stepped in, drawing back his left hand and slashing at the other's throat as he fell.

Picking up the knife, Carradine straightened. It was a long-bladed Oriental dagger, the type one usually sees adorning the walls of some old army colonel's home, a man who had seen service in the Far East. He turned it over in his hands for a moment, then stared down at the unconscious body that lay sprawled at his feet on the cobbles. He was on the point of bending and going through the other's pockets when the clatter of running feet in the alley brought him upright once again, whirling him around, his gun hand inside his coat as he recognised the two characters from the restaurant.

One of the men said swiftly: 'Relax. Forbes sent us to keep an eye on you just in case you ran into any trouble with Sen Yi.' He glanced down at the unconscious Chinese. 'Seems as though you already did, Commander.'

Carradine slowly straightened himself, nodded and relaxed a little. The two calm professional faces told him more than words or actions could have done. There was no tension or excitement there, nothing but a strange look almost of boredom. Evidently these men were used to this, just as he was.

'You know who he is?' Carradine asked.

He showed the knife. 'He tried to stick me with this. Ugly-looking thing, isn't it?'

'All depends on how you look at it, sir,' murmured the second man. 'You'll not get anything out of him when he comes round. Your best course will be to get away from here and leave him to us. We know how to deal with this type and — '

The scream from the end of the alley splintered the stillness and the tension into a thousand shrieking fragments. It was a thin, high-pitched scream that died away swiftly, leaving a silence that screamed itself on the ear.

Carradine started forward instinctively. He had taken only a couple of paces when one of the men caught at his arm and pulled him back.

'Leave this to us, Commander,' urged the other harshly. 'There is no need for you to concern yourself with this.'

'But damn it all, that could have been Sen Yi who screamed.' Impatiently, he jerked the other's hand from his arm and ran along the alley towards the restaurant. Throwing open the door, he stepped inside, looking about him as he entered.

He had fully expected a scene of panic, of men running in all directions; but there was nothing like that. Everything inside the restaurant seemed to be quite normal, yet he was certain that the scream had come from inside the place.

Three Chinese were seated at the table on the far side of the room. They lifted their heads and regarded him gravely as he burst into the room. A moment later, the bamboo curtains were drawn aside and the waiter who had served him earlier stepped through. He looked up at Carradine with a faintly surprised expression on his bland features.

'Was there something you had forgotten, sir?' he inquired politely.

'We heard a scream from here a few moments ago. I thought that there may have been an accident and I could have helped.'

'No, sir. There has been no accident.'

'But you did hear the scream?'

'I'm afraid not, sir. Perhaps it was from somewhere outside. We hear very little inside the restaurant.'

He was lying, there was no doubt about

that, Carradine told himself. Yet he knew, also, that it would be impossible for him to prove it. Those three other customers would have heard nothing either.

'I see.' He half-turned, then looked back. Was there a faint sneer in the eyes that flicked a quick glance in his direction? 'There was one thing I had forgotten.' He knew he would have to improvise here. 'Sen Yi promised me the recipe for that Chinese dish you brought me. Perhaps I could see him now.'

There was a barely perceptible pause. Then the other smiled faintly and bowed his head a little, apologetically. 'I'm afraid that this will not be possible. Sen Yi left just after you did. He will not return until after dark. Maybe if you came back tomorrow . . . '

It was this remark that triggered Carradine into deciding that the Red Dragon had already carried out its inevitable sentence of death on Sen Yi. Retribution was swift and certain as far as they were concerned. Had it been this man now standing in front of him who had, acting as an agent for the Red

Dragon, killed Sen Yi? Even if it were, he knew there would be nothing he could do to prove it. Reluctantly, he moved back towards the door. The two men were waiting for him outside, their faces grave.

'Did you find out anything?' asked one.

He shook his head. 'Sen Yi is no longer available. I'm quite sure now that it was he who screamed; that they killed him because he talked to me.'

★　★　★

The muted hum of the four powerful jets rose to the smooth, continuous whine as the Boeing 707 taxied along the perimeter track, moving towards the end of the runway. Carradine leaned back in his seat, the safety belt fastened tightly around his stomach, staring at the neck of the man seated in front of him. Turning his attention to the scene outside, he glanced through the clear perspex at the distant control building of London Airport, thought with a faint trace of nostalgia at how things had changed since the days, many years before, when those

50

buildings had been far smaller and less pretentious than they were now. In those days, there had been no whining jets, only the planes with their propellers that became glittering pools of faintly-seen light.

There was a sudden, subtle change in the sound of the engines. They had reached the end of the runway. Straining a little, he could just make it out: a wide, gleaming concrete river that stretched away as far as the eyes could see in front of the quivering plane. There was a brief pause as the engines were gunned up. He guessed that the pilot was awaiting permission to take off from Control.

The jets rose to a howling shriek, the brakes were suddenly released and they were on their way, racing along the runway like an unleashed greyhound pursuing some invisible rabbit. Three-quarters of the way along the runway, they lifted smoothly into the air, the scream of the jets fell to a muted, bearable whistle and Carradine forced himself to relax. The worst part of the journey was over, until they came within sight of Idlewild. Then there would be the long, gliding descent, with his stomach protesting at the change in altitude and his ears popping and cracking painfully. Why did the airlines not provide a drug that would dull the nerves and senses during takeoff and landing?

Leaning his head back, he loosened the belt and fixed his gaze on the ground that fell away beneath him. Five minutes later, they were above the thin, filmy air of cirrus and heading west into the wide air channel that carried the air traffic to America.

It was two days since Sen Yi had been murdered. Carradine forced the knowledge into the back of his mind, but it had the unpleasant habit of coming out and intruding on his thoughts. Sen Yi's death worried him more than most. In a way, he felt directly responsible. It was little use telling himself that he had also exposed himself to the same kind of danger; that an attempt had been made on his life just after leaving that small restaurant. He had also tried to tell himself that no matter what the reasons had been for Sen Yi coming to England, leaving behind the organisation with which he had worked in China, the other had still been a professional Secret Service agent and would have known the consequences of his actions just as well as he did himself. Perhaps Sen Yi had come to England in a last attempt to break away from that life. There had been cases that he had known of personally, of men who had wanted to get out of this dirty, hole-in-the-corner business before it sullied them completely. If so, then he had directly implicated himself again and the Red Dragon had taken its revenge on traitors.

With an effort, he told himself that he had far more important things with which to occupy his mind than the death of a Chinese agent. He was flying to America ill-prepared, knowing very little, except for the name of one man — Minden. He knew nothing of the other apart from his name. Maybe Dean could tell him a little more once he arrived in New York.

The plane droned on above the clouds. Now they were flying at twenty-five thousand feet. Through breaks in the clouds as they drifted slowly beneath the plane, he was able to see that they were still over land. Soon, the Atlantic would come into view and they would be flying over the featureless ocean for almost the whole of the journey.

They crossed the coast less than fifteen minutes later. The clouds became more and more broken as they flew over the sea, until finally they were left behind altogether; and down below was an unbroken stretch of deep blue, with the sky laying a cone of brilliance over the smooth water and the sea fading to a dull purplish haze on the skyline.

Carradine closed his eyes and settled himself more comfortably in his seat. Trying to think things out logically in his mind, he closed his thoughts to everything else but what he knew and what he would have to find out. Since Sen Yi had been brutally murdered, he felt reasonably certain that the few facts that he had learned from the other were close to the truth. The Red Dragon organisation was more widespread than even the Chief had guessed. They had discussed it the previous day. They had known that the Chinese had a counter-espionage organisation but they had never thought they were this good. The Russians they knew of old, and respected them for what they were. But the Chinese were different. How different, they were just beginning to find out, and the knowledge had come as a very unpleasant surprise to them. Small wonder, he thought wryly, that the Americans were worried.

How would the Americans react to his presence there? He knew that they were jealous of their reputation, and that there had been some occasions in the past when they had, with some justification perhaps, believed that the British Security Service could not be wholly trusted, and was not up to scratch. There would undoubtedly be some professional jealousy, some antipathy towards him. But he felt certain that he could put up with this and disregard it. It was the undeniable fact that he would be under continued observation by these men, as well as by the enemy, that was worrying him more than anything else. It might even be construed by some that he had been brought in to help because their own men had fallen down on the job. That would be the worst possible thing that could happen. Above all, he needed a free hand in his work; he needed to be able to follow his own instincts and inclinations in this matter, not be hemmed in by petty restrictions — and he foresaw only too clearly that this might happen.

But there was no point in trying to see too far ahead — his normally tidy mind had no place for that sort of mental litter. He needed a clear mind at all times.

★　　★　　★

They landed in Idlewild only a short time after they had left London, having chased the sun around the world. A little over five hours had actually elapsed, but the local time indicated they had lost only a few minutes. Following the other passengers down onto the tarmac, he walked towards customs and waited for his two suitcases to arrive from the plane. There was little formality and he was passed through quickly.

There was a fleet of taxis waiting outside the airport and he was on the point of hailing one of them when a small car glided swiftly to the edge of the sidewalk and stopped in front of him. The driver leaned his head out the window and said quietly: 'Commander Carradine?'

He nodded. The other opened his door, came around the back of the car, lifted up the boot lid and then took Carradine's cases. He stuffed them inside the boot, slammed down the boot lid again, locked it, and opened the door for him.

It was cramped for Carradine inside the car and he was forced to sit with his legs pulled up so that his knees were almost at his chest. The other switched on the ignition and said apologetically: 'Sorry about the car, but Dean thought that it would be best not to be conspicuous.'

There was a faint hint of mystery behind the friendly voice. Carradine had the feeling that things in New York were worse than he had imagined. But he made no attempt to question the other, knowing that Dean would tell him everything in good time. Settling himself back, wriggling his long-limbed body into as comfortable a position as possible, he watched the tall skyscrapers of New York glide towards him until they loomed on either side of the car. It's started, Carradine thought with a faint rise of tension in his mind. Now, very soon, he was going to catch a little more of the hell which only professional spies knew. How could one ever hope to rationalise it — this strange feeling of being utterly alone, even in the midst of a city of eight million people? The professional spy was never meant to operate in a pack. He was a lone wolf. You struck quietly and quickly, and then you ran. That was the code. If you were caught, then you had to fight it out on your own, using every possible weapon. If you lost your fight, then you died alone. In a way, it was the law of the jungle — a dirty business — and the only thing you could ever say for yourself, for the way in which you worked and lived, was that perhaps because of the thing you did, a few million people might sleep a little easier in their beds.

He lifted his gaze to the sheer rising wall of concrete and sun-glittering windows that rose on all sides of him now, shutting out the sunlight from the street. Somehow, he gained the impression that the sunlight never managed to penetrate down here onto the sidewalks, no matter what hour of the day or season of the year.

'It's a real hell-hole, isn't it?' said the man behind the wheel softly.

Carradine turned his head. 'Sorry, I'm afraid my thoughts were miles away.'

'All of this, I mean.' The other waved his hand expressively. His thick, curly hair seemed almost planned in its disarray and the strange empty blue eyes peered out at Carradine from under thick brows. Only his cruel mouth detracted from his good looks. There were odd tensions at work in this man, Carradine thought.

'I hadn't noticed,' Carradine said at length.

'You would if you had to live here,' grunted the other.

'I gather that you're not a city man yourself.'

'You bet your life I'm not. I'm from Montana. Used to having wide, open spaces around me, without all this concrete and masonry getting in the way.'

'Why stay here then?'

The other shrugged. 'I'm only here for a little while. I usually get the assignments away from here. But Dean figured that it would be best if I came along to brief you as best I can on this affair. I guess you've been told a little about it in London.' He glanced at Carradine sideways as he spoke, keeping most of his attention directed to the streaming lanes of traffic all around them.

'It was only a little. I'm hoping that Dean is able to tell me more about it. I dislike having to work in the dark as far as these people are concerned.'

'Dean's a strange man. He takes a bit of getting used to. Better go easy with him at first.' Skilfully, the other guided the car out of the mainstream of traffic, eased it into the kerb, and switched off the ignition the second he took the car out of gear. 'Here we are,' he said cheerfully. 'I'll take you up. He is expecting you but I

60

better check first with our Control.'

They went inside the tall building, through a wide, arched entrance, along a short corridor, and paused in front of the elevator. Carradine's companion thumbed a button on the wall and a few moments later the elevator slid smoothly down from one of the upper floors. The steel grille opened noiselessly and the other motioned Carradine to go inside.

'Top floor, I'm afraid,' he said, smiling faintly. 'Another whim of Dean's.'

The elevator began its smooth upward climb. Several floors flashed in front of Carradine's gaze but he soon lost count of them. Once the elevator came to a stop, there were more corridors, wide and airy, with large windows here and there that looked out over the tops of the nearby buildings. It surprised him a little to see how high they were. Finally, the other stopped outside a glass-panelled door and pressed one of three buttons on the wall. There was no sound, no flashing lights; but a few moments later, the door opened silently in front of them.

3

The Merchants of Death

Dean shook his hand carefully and motioned to the red plush chair fronting the long, expensive desk. 'Have a good flight over?' he inquired. The pleasant, drawling voice went well with the fleshy features. Carradine guessed that he came from one of the southern states, possibly Texas.

He sat down in the chair and stretched out his legs straight in front of him, quite relaxed. There was a pause, then Dean lifted his head and went on: 'Did Arland give you any idea of our problem here?' He glanced at the man who had brought Carradine there as he spoke.

Carradine shook his head. 'No one seems to know very much about this trouble. I was hoping you might be able to enlighten me a little.'

'Yes, indeed,' Dean murmured. For a

long moment he stared off into space, seemingly lost in thought. The deep-set eyes appeared to hood themselves like those of a bird of prey. Carradine, watching him closely from beneath lowered lids, guessed that there were hidden depths in this man, not noticeable to most men, which explained why he had held down this particular job.

'I've heard quite a lot about you, Carradine. Everything I've heard indicates that you are the man we need for this job.' He smiled thinly. 'I suppose that to you, all of this is purely routine.'

'I've learned from past experience that in this kind of work nothing is routine. The man who thinks that way is soon dead.'

'I guess you're right at that.' Dean flicked a quick enigmatic glance at Arland, standing near the wall.

Carradine followed the other's gaze, then switched his glance to the small table behind Dean. He had noticed it casually when he had first entered the room, but now he saw that there was a small tape-recorder on it and the microphone was somewhere behind Dean's broad back, invisible to him. The tape spools were rotating slowly. American official-dom and security were certainly taking no chances with Steve Carradine, he thought wryly.

Sitting back in his chair, Dean said quickly: 'As from this moment, you will be working for me and until this job is finished, you will have nothing whatever to do with London. This has already been agreed between your Government and mine. You'll be on open salary here — within certain limits of course. We don't want you spending thousands of dollars, natu-rally, but we do want you to have everything you need.'

'I see.'

'Officially you'll be based here. I have arranged for you to have an office in this building. This is the nerve centre of operations. We have radio-teleprinter links all over the country, and with one or two selected countries abroad. All signals will be encoded. You will have to act in close liaison with the Code and Cypher Division. Arland will introduce you to them.'

'Fine — but what exactly is the job?' Carradine asked.

Dean heaved himself from his chair, then walked over to one of the wall maps, beckoning Carradine to follow him. Carradine moved over to the map. Dean was pointing to a spot in New Mexico.

'Right here,' he said in a cold, matter-of-fact voice, 'one of our top security men was killed a little over a month ago. He was carrying certain extremely vital documents relating to the defence centres we have in this area here.' The other's stubby finger moved a little. 'Ordinarily, had this been simply an isolated incident, we would merely have left it to the FBI to investigate. As it turned out, it was the first in a series of apparently isolated, but now quite obviously interrelated incidents.' He turned his head slowly and stared bleakly at Carradine.

'The Red Dragon,' Carradine said softly.

'That's right. How did you manage to get on to them?'

'I met a man in London who had

worked with them for some years before he escaped from Red China via Hong Kong.'

'And he talked?' There was a note of surprise in the other's voice.

'I'm afraid he was silenced — permanently — just after talking to me. He was able to tell me very little, I'm afraid.'

Dean nodded. He moved over to the window. His thick horn-rimmed glasses winked briefly as he turned and said: 'The police picked a hobo out of an alley in the Bronx last night. Odd thing about him. He wasn't drunk as they figured at first. He had been drugged — and we now know he is one of our top security men from the missile proving grounds in New Mexico. We've known for some time now that there's a Red organisation in America working to find the location of our nuclear defence posts. This man of ours was after the top men in that organisation.' He paused and lowered his gaze on to Carradine. 'As from today, Mr. Carradine, so are you.'

He walked back to the desk and lowered himself into the chair. 'You know,

I sit here in this air-conditioned office like some figurative bloated spider, giving orders to more than three dozen agents scattered throughout the whole length and breadth of the country, and each time I give a man an order I have the feeling I've just signed his death warrant. I suppose that in any less a man that would be enough to stop him from sleeping at nights.' He sounded almost apologetic.

Carradine grinned faintly. 'Someone has to do that kind of work. I'm afraid it wouldn't appeal to me.'

'I can understand that.' Inwardly Dean was thinking that the British Secret Service chose their killers well. There was something about this man seated opposite him — a kind of quiet inner ruthlessness that spoke volumes about the other. He guessed that Carradine was a man who did not like killing simply for the sake of killing, but who would destroy a man without a qualm or hesitation should the necessity ever arise. Bringing his hands down, he looked straight across at Carradine. 'You can start by having a talk with the security man. At the moment he's in the hospital five blocks from here. If they've managed to do anything with him, he may be able to talk. Frankly, I wouldn't bank too heavily on it. It's just an off-chance.'

'I'll do that.' Carradine rose to his feet, then paused. 'By the way, can you give me any dope on a man named Minden?'

Dean's eyes took on a hard, foxy look. He said: 'I've heard the name before. If we have any record at all on the man it will be in the files.' He leaned over to one side and pushed a red button on the desk.

The intercom buzzed for a moment and then a voice said: 'Central registry.'

'Dean here, Clive. See if you can get me anything on a man named Minden. I've an idea we came across him about nine months or a year ago. Let me have it as soon as possible.'

'Five minutes, sir,' said the voice at the other end of line. There was a sharp click as the connection was broken.

Dean sat back. 'A good man, that. If the information is there, he'll have it out within minutes. Got a mind like a computer. Photographic memory and all that.'

The information arrived in four minutes. The intercom buzzed and Dean flicked down a switch. 'Yes?'

'Clive here, sir. That information you wanted. Carl Minden. He's a German, came to the States nine years ago. There was evidence that he was connected with the Helleren case four years ago, but he dropped out of sight before he could be arrested and brought to trial. We thought he may have been spirited back to Europe, but there was no proof of this.'

Dean flicked a quick glance in Carradine's direction. The other nodded and said in a soft tone: 'He's still here in the States, working for the Red Dragon.'

Dean wagged his head and said into the intercom: 'We believe that he's still in this country, Clive. Probably working for the Reds.'

'The Russians?' queried the voice.

'No — the Chinese.'

There was a faint whistle of surprise over the intercom. 'I see. You want me to try to dig any further on this, sir? Sounds as though we are a little behind the times with this particular file.'

'If you would, Clive. In the meantime, we'll get on to it from this end.' He broke the connection and looked up at Carradine, then across to where Arland stood leaning against the wall. 'You got anything on him, Bill?'

Arland shook his head. 'Naturally I heard about the Helleren affair. But the name Minden means nothing to me, I'm afraid.'

'From what I recall of him,' went on Dean musingly, almost as though he had not heard the other's statement, 'he's a nasty piece of work. Worked for the SS before and during the war. How he escaped justice is a wonder to me. He must be a bright lad, otherwise he would never have survived as long as this with half the police forces in the West looking for him. I doubt if the Germans have completely forgotten about him. A lot of those men changed from the Nazi party into good, first-class citizens as soon as the war ended and they realized what lay in store for them once the Allies started meting out justice. Even now, all these years later, they still aren't completely safe, not even if they manage to get into South America. Remember what happened to Reichmann. It could happen just as easily to Minden and he knows it. But he's in with a good organisation if your information happens to be correct. You got it from this Red Dragon agent?'

'That's right. It was the only piece of positive information he was able to give me.'

'So at the moment, wherever he is, he believes himself to be safe.' Dean studied the other for a long moment, then said briskly: 'All right. You'd better get along to the hospital and see if Wellman is any condition to talk. Arland will show you the way.'

Carradine nodded. Arland pushed himself away from the wall and followed him to the door. Opening it, Carradine paused as Dean said: 'One other thing, Carradine. No doubt you have realized by now that your greatest asset to us is that although these people may know most of my agents by sight, they don't know you. Because of this, you will be in command of this operation, directly responsible only to me. Arland knows the situation. Don't try to get in touch with me. If you have any important information, ring the number that Arland will give you. It will be redirected to me via the Coding and Cypher Department.'

'I understand.' Carradine closed the door slowly. His last picture of Dean was of the other lighting a cigar, sitting back in his chair, head tilted back a little, staring up at the ceiling through half-closed eyes. To all outward appearances, he seemed to be a man without a trouble or care in the world. Carradine grinned wryly to himself as he followed Arland along the corridor. Only the few who really knew him could guess at the turmoil that must be raging inside the other's mind.

★ ★ ★

The doctor was a young, fresh-looking man in his early thirties, looking spruce and efficient in his white suit. He walked a couple of inches ahead of Carradine as he led the way along the wide, well-lit passage that smelled of antiseptic and other vague and indefinable odours. They were making their way towards the wide double doors of the ward at the far end of the corridor.

'This is an odd case, Mr. Carradine,' said the other quietly. 'He was admitted late last night after being found in some alley down in the Bronx. Naturally, we get many such cases from that area. Bottle fights, knife fights, and any kind of weapon you can imagine. They sometimes come in ones, more often in threes and fours. We suspected that he was drunk, but we soon discovered that he was under the influence of a drug.'

'Do you know which drug it was?'

'They're still checking on that at the moment. I'd say it was probably one of the sodium pentothal type.'

'One of the truth drugs?'

'It would appear so. Once we received word that he was working for the Government — the Department of Defence, I understand — we had him immediately transferred to a private ward. All the staff assigned to his case have been security checked.'

Carradine eyed the other's broad back for a moment as the doctor pushed open the door of the ward with the flat of his hand. There were screens around the bed in the small, airy room. A nurse, seated in the chair in one corner glanced up quickly as they came in, laid down the chart on which she had been marking lines in red ink, got to her feet and came forward, flashing them both a brilliant smile.

'This is Mr. Carradine,' explained the doctor. 'He is working with one of the Government departments.'

The nurse nodded, but said nothing.

'Is he conscious yet?' asked the doctor.

'He came out of the coma temporarily for a few minutes about three quarters of an hour ago. Doctor Thornton had a look at him, but the improvement was only temporary, I'm afraid.'

The other nodded. Waiting until they had pulled aside the screens, he motioned Carradine forward, following close on his heels. The man lying on the bed seemed so still beneath the thin sheets that for a moment it seemed difficult for Carradine to believe that he was still alive. Then, looking closer, he saw the sheet rising and falling slowly and shallowly.

The doctor checked the man's pulse, then lifted one of the closed eyelids, and let it drop back into place. He sighed softly. 'I'm afraid you're going to be out of luck, Mr. Carradine.'

'Can you give me any idea at all when he is likely to come out of this coma?'

'None at all, I'm afraid. It could be an hour or so, or perhaps days before he is in any fit condition to talk coherently.'

'This drug you think has been used on him. Would that have the effect of taking away his memory?'

'Partial amnesia? Somehow, I doubt it. We can only wait until he comes round and then — '

'Doctor!' The nurse, standing beside the bed, spoke sharply. Carradine turned his head. The patient's eyes were open, staring up at the ceiling — wide, curiously flat, and empty. The doctor moved forward and bent over his patient as Carradine moved to the foot of the bed, watching closely. Slowly, the patient's eyes moved — not in the direction of the white-coated man standing over him, but downward so that his gaze travelled across the length of the bed, locking with Carradine's. There was no recognition in them, but quite suddenly, Carradine saw the expression that gusted over the man's face, the look at the back of the wide-open eyes.

It was an expression he had seen many times before, on countless faces. The hunted look, compounded of fear, terror and the knowledge that from this particular nightmare there was no possible escape. Thrusting down with his hands, he started up from the bed, a faint, low cry escaping from his grimacing lips.

'Take it easy,' said the doctor in a soothing tone. 'This is a hospital. You're quite safe now.'

The look of terror did not ease as he tried to force words from between his trembling lips. 'The Red — ' The hoarse voice faded into silence as the other's head fell back onto the pillow. He seemed utterly spent by the effort.

'What was that?' asked the doctor. He bent lower, trying to pick out any further words.

Brushing past the nurse, Carradine moved to the man, placed his face close to his. 'Go on with what you were trying to say,' he said forcefully, urgently. 'The Red Dragon. They did this, didn't they?'

With an effort, the other nodded his head. On the top of the sheet, the fingers curled into taut talons, nails biting deeply into the flesh of the palms, but he did not seem to notice it.

'Now try to think carefully. What happened? Who did this to you? Do you know any names? People, places — anything?'

The other squeezed his eyes shut as if trying to keep out the sight of something unutterably horrible. The doctor leaned over and caught Carradine by the arm. 'It's no use. Either he can't recall anything, or he can't tell you. I think we had better let him get some rest. Maybe in a day or so, he will be able to tell you all you want to know and — '

'In this dirty business, doctor,' Carradine said tightly, 'even a day or two can be too long. We are fighting a dangerous enemy. Once they discover that he is still alive, they'll find a way to silence him — permanently.'

'He'll be quite safe so long as he is in hospital and under our care,' said the other stiffly.

'Don't you believe it,' Carradine said with a touch of sarcasm in his voice. 'I know these people and it's evident from that remark that you don't. They can get a man anywhere. Even here. Now — ' He turned his attention back to the man in the bed, shaking off the doctor's restraining grip. 'Tell me what you can. For God's sake — try!'

At length the lips moved again, eyes still wide and staring. Then the words, spaced and slurred, the syllables all running together, came out through the shaking lips. 'Socorro . . . careful, man called Cornish . . . top secret information. Urgent see Dean . . . ' The voice trailed off into silence and the other lay back, his eyes closed, seemingly exhausted.

The doctor said sharply: 'I'm afraid I shall have to insist that you let him rest now; I'm not sure that I ought to have allowed you to do that.'

'I had no choice,' Carradine said shortly. 'This is something far bigger than you can possibly imagine. Even the life of this man here is nothing compared to it.'

'So?' The other looked at him in mild surprise. 'And what does that piece of information convey to you? Anything at all?'

'I'm not sure. At least it gives me something to go on.'

*   *   *

The city of Socorro in central New Mexico lay on the west bank of the Rio Grande River, some seventy-five miles south of Albuquerque at the junction of US Highways 85 and 60. Carradine motored comfortably along the broad highway in the light afternoon sunshine. He kept his eyes open as he drove, knowing that this time he could not afford to make any mistakes. Even though

Dean seemed sure that he would not be recognised by any members of the Red Dragon organisation operating inside the United States, Carradine did not deem it quite certain. That poor devil back in the hospital in New York . . .

He let his mind linger on that for a moment. Why hadn't they killed him while there had been the chance? Evidently the pentothal-type drugs had been used to obtain information from him. Now the Red Dragon would know everything that had been tucked away in the security of that man's mind. But why let him remain alive? Carradine found himself worrying over this point, incongruous as it seemed. There was one answer, nibbling away at the edges of his brain like a tiny grey mouse; but it was one he did not want to admit.

Just suppose that these people were one jump ahead of the FBI. Suppose they had already figured out that they might send for someone known to no one in the States. One way of discovering his identity would be to lay a trap for him, lure him down here after implanting this information in the mind of that man who had been found in the alley out in the Bronx . . .

Better keep his eyes and ears open once he arrived here. Dean had warned him over the telephone that the nearest American defence site lay less than fifty miles from Socorro and that it had been less than ten miles north of the city that one of their security men from the missile base had been found in a wrecked car, his briefcase containing several vital documents missing.

He drove now along the bank of the wide river, glinting in the sunlight. Far off in the distance, over to the west, he could make out the tall, undulating peaks of the Socorro and Magdalena mountains. It was a peaceful scene, totally unlike that which he had been imagining in his mind as he had driven down from Albuquerque. Socorro was evidently in the centre of a grain and dairying region. There was little evidence of any military establishment close by. He drove through an area of orchards stretching away on either side of the broad horizon, the trees now showing red and gold in their autumn attire. Sitting back a little in his seat, he relaxed, playing with his thoughts, still not having made up his mind on the line he intended to take once he reached the city.

There was his man Minden, who seemed to be the mastermind in this part of the country. He had already decided that Cornish was merely an operator, possibly in a high position of trust, able to get information without giving himself away or arousing any suspicion.

The Red Dragon would undoubtedly have worked with the patience character-istic of the Oriental mind. They would move so slowly and carefully in the beginning that no suspicion would be formed in the minds of anyone. Only now, when they possibly considered themselves strong enough, was there any urgency in their dealings. Maybe it all had something to do with the disturbing fact that China had now exploded her second atomic bomb and there seemed little doubt that they had mastered the technique of evolving and building atomic weapons. How long it would be before they reached parity with the West was problematical. But in the meantime, they needed to know every detail about the Western defence system, the exact whereabouts of their missile sites and methods of operation. Then, when the time came and they were ready to put into operation their plan for world conquest, they would be able to strike first and destroy the American capacity to retaliate.

It was a numbing and terrifying thought. How soon would that day come? The trouble was that they were getting very little reliable information out of China. If they only had an idea what they were doing, they might know just how much time they had. The Section had one or two men working inside China at the present time, but their difficulties were, quite naturally, virtually insurmountable. He himself did not envy any of those men.

Carradine stepped on the accelerator. There was a sudden sense of urgency in his mind. He could now make out the city in the distance. In the yellow glow of sunlight it all looked peaceful enough. A ripple of grim amusement went through him at the thought. It was the places that looked so quiet and peaceful that turned out to hold the most danger for him.

The feeling persisted, growing stronger as he drove in through the open outskirts of the town. On the face of it, Socorro was just a normal, average American city — he guessed the population was somewhere in the region of five thousand — dominated by the fine buildings of the New Mexico Institute of Mining and Technology. It was plainly an agricultural city, although it had become the largest city in the New Mexico Territory during the 1880s because of the silver, which had been discovered close by. Mining had become intermittent after the steep drop in the price of silver at the end of the last century and now there was only a little done, mainly for hydrocarbons and zinc.

He located a five-storey hotel halfway along the wide thoroughfare and pulled into the parking lot alongside the building. There was plenty of room for the car, there being only four others in the lot, and he guessed that there would be very few visitors here at this time of the year. He had felt a little surprise, driving into the city, at not seeing any sign of military personnel. Since this was one of the largest cities in the vicinity, he had expected to find it well patronised.

The hotel was all that he had expected — reasonably cheap, modern and clean, with excellent service. Carradine had a hot bath, changed, and then made his way downstairs and ate an excellent meal. His room was on the third floor. Why they had put him there when it was obvious there were scarcely any other guests in the hotel, he did not know. Possibly, he thought, it was something to do with keeping all floors occupied during the slack periods. Still, he did not grumble. The view from his window was magnificent. For several minutes he stood and stared out towards the west, to where the sun was beginning to dip towards the mountains that stood out on the skyline in a wide band of blue and purple, with the reds and golds lying stretched out behind them, a perfect contrast in colours.

Inwardly, he felt tense. Perhaps if he took a walk around the city until it got dark, it might help. He made his way downstairs, handed his key to the clerk behind the reception desk, and walked over to the wide glass doors. The sunlight laid a red glow on them, almost as if there were a huge fire burning outside.

Pushing them open with the flat of his hand, he was on the point of letting them swing back into place when he caught the faint scent of perfume behind him, and turned sharply. The girl stood a few inches away, her gaze cool and speculative on him. He had noticed her at dinner, seated at one of the tables near the wide windows that overlooked the ground at the rear of the hotel. Stepping aside, he held the door open for her. She gave a sideways, appraising look, and paused on the wide steps.

'Thank you.' Her voice was soft, with the faint drawl of the South. 'You arrived this afternoon, didn't you?'

He nodded. 'From Albuquerque. The end of a long drive from New York.'

The delicately pencilled brows lifted

slightly. 'Then you must be a long way from home. Do you know Socorro?'

Carradine shrugged. 'Only the part I saw on the way in. I was going to take a look around before dark.'

'There's really very little to see.' She looked at him gravely, evidently considering him. 'Would you think it forward of me if I offered to show you the few sights worth looking at in the city?'

'Not at all. I can't imagine a more charming guide.' He fell into step beside her, watching her most closely now. Although she was an exceptionally beautiful girl, she was the kind who did not need to watch her beauty, which came quite naturally to her. The dark hair provided the perfect contrast to the pale oval of her face. Her skin glowed with a healthy tan, the red blood pulsing under the flesh. There was an air of self-reliance about her stance and the way she walked, with determination and independence in the set of her jaw and the high cheekbones.

They turned into the main street. The first of the inevitable neon lights were flicking on along the storefronts.

'My name is Candy Vance — it's short for Candida.' A pause, then she glanced at him impishly. 'Are you here on business, Mr. Carradine? Or is it pleasure? New Mexico can be very beautiful and relaxing at this time of the year.'

He tried to show neither surprise nor alarm. Instead, he said quietly: 'And how is it that you know my name?'

'Quite simple. I looked in the register at the hotel. There are only a few others there. The elderly married couple I noticed at once, and you don't look like a Mr. Schwartzheimer. So I put you down as Mr. Carradine.'

'I see.' Her explanation was so simple that he told himself it had to be the truth. Yet that little germ of suspicion was still running around the grey edges of his mind. 'Business and pleasure,' he said, wondering inwardly how much he could trust this girl. 'I'm looking for a friend of mine. Last I heard of him he was living here; I told him I'd look him up if I ever came to these parts.'

'Perhaps I know him.'

It was all said so quietly and innocently that there seemed to be no other reason behind the question than a mere genuine desire to help. He shrugged slightly. 'His name is Cornish. I don't suppose that — ?'

'Albert Cornish?' There was a sudden sharp edge to the girl's tone. Then she controlled herself. 'Of course. He's one of the top officials at the Institute.'

4

Kill or Cure

It was the sort of office usually reserved for the presidents of large American business corporations or film magnates: of large but pleasing proportions, with plenty of glass to admit and reflect the sunlight. The deep purple carpet sat at least three inches beneath Carradine's feet as he walked in. The pert secretary flashed him a quick smile, then backed out of the room, closing the door gently behind her.

Carradine looked about him in faint surprise. The paintings on the walls were obviously originals. He had, on a few occasions, seen canvasses such as these auctioned at Sotheby's for several thousand pounds each. Evidently Albert Cornish was a man with very expensive tastes and the kind of money with which to pander to them. The sixty-four thousand dollar question was: By what means did he get the money that enabled him to live in this luxury?

The broad mahogany desk stood just in front of the wide window and looked out over the rolling green orchard country to the south-west of Socorro. The air in the room was fresh, cool and slightly scented, and there was a very faint hum of air conditioning fans whirring softly in the ceiling somewhere out of sight.

While Carradine was taking in the scene, there came the soft click of a door opening and, turning swiftly, he saw the man enter the room and move forward.

'Mr. Carradine?' murmured the other quietly. He held out his hand, shook the other firmly, then moved around the side of the desk, motioning Carradine to the other chair. 'Please sit down. I'm afraid I'm not quite sure of the exact nature of your business.' He pushed the box of cigars across the desk, waited until Carradine had taken one, and then lit one for himself, blowing the smoke high into the air, his head thrown back. The friendly smile was still there on his lips, but it had not penetrated to his eyes. They regarded Carradine closely from beneath lowered lids, wide and empty, devoid of all emotion.

'It's of a rather confidential nature,' Carradine said soberly. 'I trust that you will keep everything under your hat.'

'That goes without saying,' said the other, his features still expressionless.

'Briefly, I'm carrying out a broad survey of this area for one of the Government departments. Naturally, I am not at liberty to say which one, but I came to you since I understand that in your capacity here, you were of great help to them on some previous occasion.'

Cornish's eyes widened a fraction, but this, and the very faint tremor of his hand as he leaned forward and gently tapped the length of grey ash from his cigar, were the only indications of his thoughts at that moment. He said very cautiously: 'Obviously you have a great deal of information about me which could be known only to a very few people.' He pushed his chair back a couple of inches, rose to his feet and paced towards the window, standing for a few moments with his back to Carradine, staring intently out of the room, down into the gardens below. At length, he turned. 'I hope you will forgive me asking this, Mr. Carradine,' he said smoothly. 'But do you mind showing me your credentials before I answer any more of your questions? Not that I am doubting your statements, of course, but in this business one has to be very careful.'

You're damned right on that point, thought Carradine grimly. He fished inside his pocket and brought out the carefully prepared documents with which he had been provided by Dean's office. Cornish took them, studied them with a thoughtful glance, then handed them back, clearly satisfied.

'I must admit to being surprised, but I shall do anything in my power to assist you. What is it that you want to know?'

Carradine sat back. He had of course no way of telling whether the other would be lying or not. His only course now was to go on probing until something clicked into place. Inwardly, there was a feeling that Cornish was beginning to become uneasy. It was visible in several little things: the faint twitching of the tiny muscle high in his left cheek just below the eye, and the way in which he flicked the grey ash from his cigar more frequently than was necessary. Maybe he could push the other to the point where events would force him to a rash decision. Already, he guessed that Cornish was only a middleman in this vast organisation, this network of men spread through the entire length and breadth of the United States. He was important because he could get his hands on confidential information regarding the men who worked at the secret missile base in southern New Mexico, and do so without arousing the slightest suspicion. If that drugged man back in New York had not muttered his name and that of this town, he might have got away with it for long enough.

'I believe that you helped the Department of Defence when they were planning the sites for their defensive missile sites in this territory.'

Cornish nodded. 'That is perfectly true. We were asked to cooperate with them in choosing the most ideal sites, geologically speaking.'

'And you were given free access to these various places?'

'Why — yes.' Cornish's smile widened a little, but Carradine's sharp eyes noticed the faint sheen of perspiration that had formed on the man's forehead. He's scared already, he thought with a grim amusement. Maybe it would be best if he came right out with the real reason for him being there, let Cornish know just how much he really did know about him, and accuse him to his face of being in league with the Red Dragon. Almost as soon as the thought crossed his mind, he rejected it.

The people who were behind him, held him in a grip of steel. It was extremely doubtful if Cornish would talk, even if he was scared to the point of death; and even if he would, whether he could tell Carradine anything of real importance about this sordid business.

'I see.' Carradine spoke the words

carefully. The little muscle ticked again in Cornish's cheek. Evidently a tell-tale sign as far as the other was concerned. He let the silence drag for several minutes.

At length Cornish said: 'I'm afraid that I don't quite see the trend of this conversation, Mr. Carradine.' He spread his hands in an apologetic motion on top of the desk. 'Is there some doubt in the Department of Defence about the manner in which I have been working on this particular project?'

'None at all. But there have been incidents — I won't bore you with the details of them — which have made it imperative that everyone connected with the projects must be questioned.'

'I hope you realize just how many things you're setting in motion now that you have undertaken this mission,' said the other dryly.

Carradine shrugged his shoulders. 'I'm afraid if we stopped to think about that every time, we would get nothing done and the security of this country would be virtually non-existent. This is purely routine work.'

Stiffly, Cornish said: 'And I presume that I have to answer your questions. That is, unless I want to be hauled in front of one of your committees and questioned there.'

'At the moment, that necessity doesn't arise,' Carradine said evenly. 'I won't say that it won't happen in the future. You're quite at liberty to say nothing — as of now.' His tone left no doubt as to the real meaning behind his words.

'I think I'm beginning to understand.' Cornish nodded. He sat forward a little, hunched in his chair. 'I'm afraid there is nothing I can tell you. I worked for the Government when the defence sites were erected. They needed expert advice on the nature of the strata on which they intended to build their surface erections, and also sink their defence installations, keeping the rockets with their nuclear warheads far underground.'

'And you have divulged none of this information to anyone else?'

'Absolutely not,' declared the other. The faint sheen of sweat which Carradine had noticed earlier had now begun to coalesce into tiny drops on his forehead.

Carradine leaned forward across the desk, not taking his eyes off the other for a single instant. He deliberately waited again for several moments. Outside, there was the sound of the heavy truck moving along the highway. It faded quickly. 'You're perfectly right in what you're thinking,' he said, his voice very soft. 'There has been a leak of information concerning the defence sites. We have to check every possible source.'

'Of course. I understand.' The other's attitude of complacent assuredness had drained swiftly from him. At the back of his eyes and visible in the set of his jaw were the unmistakable signs of a hunted animal. He was clearly doing his best not to show this to Carradine.

'Good.' Carradine straightened. 'I think I've taken up too much of your valuable time, Mr. Cornish. I trust that you will forgive me. But you know how these things are where the Government is concerned.'

Cornish rose a little uncertainly to his feet. His handshake was a little limp. He showed Carradine to the door, closing it behind him. As he made his way along the airy, well-lit corridor, Carradine smiled grimly to himself. If that little performance hadn't started things moving, then nothing short of a hydrogen bomb would. He wondered when, and how, Cornish would make his next move. Whether he would now get in touch with his superior — possibly Minden — and discuss this new development with him; whether he would try to work things out himself.

He shrugged his shoulders as he walked out of the imposing building, and made his way along the flower-bordered drive. Sufficient unto that day was the evil thereof, he thought with a grim amusement. As he reached the end of the drive, he paused, turned, and glanced back at the building to where the window of Cornish's room was situated. He saw a dim shadow move away from the glass, stepping back swiftly into the room. So Cornish was watching him, making certain that he had left, had not hung around to find out anything more. Well, he could afford to give him a little time to think things over, to stretch his nerves to breaking point. It would only serve to make him act more rashly than otherwise. If he could make Cornish act impulsively, without rational thought, all the better.

* * *

When he got back to his room at the hotel, he was only mildly surprised to find that everything had been searched. Whoever had been through his room had certainly known his job. Outwardly, there was no evidence that his belongings had been touched, but there were little things which told him quite clearly that someone had been there, had examined everything there and then replaced the individual items as closely as possible in the positions they had earlier occupied. Only to his trained eye were the tiny discrepancies noticeable.

Lowering his long body into the chair by the window, he lit a cigarette and smoked it slowly as he turned things over in his mind. Whoever had done this while he had been talking with Cornish had found nothing. There had been no incriminating evidence anywhere in what he had brought with him that would have told these men anything about him. It was just possible, of course, that the Red Dragon was taking no chances, that they went through this procedure with every stranger who arrived in the town.

But it meant that he was close to them, far closer than he had imagined when he had visited Cornish. He finished the cigarette, stubbed out the butt in the tray, then left the hotel, picking up his car from the parking lot. The sun was high, the air warm and clear, and it seemed an ideal time for a leisurely drive through the countryside in the direction of the southern border.

The girl's white sports car was in the parking lot as he drove out. His feelings about her were oddly confused and there was a nagging sense of impatience within him at this confusion. He sensed that there was something more to her being in Socorro at this time and the way in which they had been thrown together, but she had been oddly reticent about this and he

101

had not pressed her to answer any of the burning questions in his mind.

A pity she hadn't been around in the hotel. He could think of nothing more pleasant than for her to accompany him on a drive through the delightful country-side around Socorro,

Ten miles out of the city he turned off the major highway, taking a narrower road which led him towards the mountains that loomed high on the skyline. The road here was deserted and he stepped on the accelerator, enjoying the sensation of speed. The open ground on either side of the road swept past him in a blur of grey and green. Gradually he found himself climbing, and there were sharply angled bends in the road which forced him to ease up on the accelerator pedal, the needle of the speedometer falling slowly until it hovered steadily around the fifty mark. On his right, there was a steep precipice that fell from close on three hundred feet into a rocky stretch of ground. On the bends, the road had been widened to allow plenty of room for two vehicles to pass; but on the short, straight stretches, it was barely wide enough for one car to pass another.

Here and there, on the lower slopes of the foothills, he was able to make out large square plots of cultivated ground on which orchards had been established. The trees, spaced out in even rows like soldiers on parade, were hung heavily with fruit. It would be a bumper crop this particular year, he thought. At this altitude the air was as clear as wine, and in spite of the faint purplish haze in the distance which obscured some of the further details, he was able to see for close on seventy miles, out to where the rocky ground gave way to more open desert country.

Swinging the car on one of the sharp corners, he caught a brief glimpse of the other car behind him, moving swiftly up the twisting mountain road. Had it not been in just the right position on one of the straight stretches of road, he would have missed it completely. He watched it in the mirror for a moment: a dark red saloon car, hugging the road as it swung around one of the bends. Whoever was behind the wheel clearly knew this road and was an excellent driver. He judged that the car was travelling well over seventy miles an hour, gaining on him rapidly.

A moment later, the car was lost to view. Gently, he pushed down on the accelerator, leaned forward and opened the glove compartment, checking that the heavy Luger was there. It was just possible that Cornish had worked faster than he had expected. Maybe he judged that Carradine was a more dangerous enemy than any of the others who had come snooping around and wanted to get rid of him as soon as possible, in order to safeguard his own position.

He did a controlled skid around one of the corners, sucking a gust of air sharply into his lungs as the car side-swiped violently and slid dangerously close to the edge of the road. He had the feeling that one of the wheels actually went over the edge and had hung there spinning for a split second before the car managed to right itself. In spite of the sense of danger crowding swiftly on him, Carradine felt some of the life begin to come back into his body — the sense of sheer excitement heightening his reflexes, sending the blood surging through his veins. How far this road continued before there was any branching off it, he did not know. He guessed that it probably went straight through the narrow pass, which he could just see whenever he swung around one of the corners, then on down the other side, before there were any diversions. His only chance was to stay well ahead of them.

He wound down the window and felt the rush of cool air against his face. Swinging around a corner, he came upon a long stretch of road that climbed steeply, but virtually straight, for three miles or so, clear up to the pass he had noticed earlier. Setting his teeth, he pressed hard on the accelerator. The car responded warmly and seemed to leap forward, tyres screeching on the fine grit on the road surface. As he drove, he kept a sharp lookout in the mirror, watching for the moment when the other car came into sight around the bend. This would tell him how much of a lead he had; might even force him to alter his plans.

He swore softly under his breath as the saloon swung into sight scarcely a mile behind him. They had made excellent time and had overhauled him with ease. What kind of engine had they got under the bonnet of the car? he wondered. It was just possible, too, that the other had chains on the tyres, which could explain why they had managed to keep to the road so well on the corners.

The tall pinnacles of rock on either side of the pass rushed towards him. They blotted out the streaming sunlight as he swept through them. Then he was out into the open again, on the downgrade. The road ahead twisted into a series of S-bends again, and less than a mile away it ran through a narrow bridge across a steep-sided ravine. Carradine's mind raced furiously on the problem of shaking off the pursuit.

He knew the other car must be gaining fast, but he did not have the advantage of knowing every twist and bend of the road, or of having chains on the wheels, possibly even Rally studs. Forced to slow down as he ran into the first of the

S-bends, he saw that the saloon was gaining on him rapidly now, less than half a mile distant. In the mirror, in the clear air, he was able to distinguish the three shapes in it, the pale blur of the driver's face hunched over the wheel.

Oddly, now that he recognized what he was up against, Carradine felt calm. The problem of what he had to do was a problem no longer. His hands sat lightly and delicately on the wheel as he eased the car around the bend. The camber was set badly, almost in the wrong direction, and he felt the car lurch and sway as it hit the bend. The fencing alongside the lead into the bridge loomed up on him and for a second he had the feeling that he was travelling too fast for the turn — that he was bound to skid, completely out of control, and smash through the flimsy fencing, the car turning over and over in the air, striking the sharp needles of rock on the way down until it piled up in a smashed, tangled ruin, several hundred feet below.

His fingers tightened convulsively on the wheel and swung it gently, taking care not to over-correct as he felt the rear wheels begin their inevitable slide on the treacherous stony surface of the road. It was a normal reflex movement, easing up on the accelerator and keeping his foot away from the brake, which could so easily have been fatal. Even so, the wooden uprights scraped against the side of the car as he swept past them with less than an inch to spare. His skin crawled as he passed over the narrow bridge. Down below him, on both sides, the gaping mouth of the ravine yawned hungrily. With an easy sway of his body and hands, coordinating every movement with no unnecessary actions, he drove over the bridge, into the rocks on the far side. Behind him, the red saloon screamed down on the bridge, lurching out of the S-bend, tyres screeching as the driver fought to control the car.

A swift glance in the mirror and Carradine saw the man beside the driver lean out of the window, ignoring the rails which flashed by within inches of his body. The sunlight, shafting through the rocky teeth on the side of the road, glinted off the gun in his hand.

No doubt now what these men were after. Veering over to the left-hand side of the road, praying that there was no other car heading towards him, Carradine cut the corner with scant inches to spare. He sat hunched forward, shoulder blades tensed. Savagely, he fought to relax. A shoulder was no use against the slamming impact of a .45 slug, he told himself fiercely.

The bullet struck the side of the car and ricocheted off with a shrill whine that was clearly audible even above the roar of the engine. There was another shot and the window behind him suddenly crazed over, a ragged hole in the centre of the splintered area where the slug had penetrated. Carradine felt the breath of it close to his head as it buried itself in the dashboard. Desperately, he fought to control the car. By deliberately swinging it from side to side along the narrow road, he was able to prevent the other car from drawing level with him and forcing him off the road, a manoeuvre that was clearly these men's intention.

He shot out of a bend into a straight stretch. Too late, he saw the warning sign by the side of the road. Less than three hundred yards beyond it lay rocks which had at some recent time slid down the side of the mountain, engulfing half the road. There were a couple of red lights placed twenty feet from the pile of rocks. Automatically, Carradine slammed on the brakes, gripping the wheel tightly to lock it on a straight course. At this speed, he could not possibly hope to miss all of these rocks; but with a fantastic amount of luck, he might manage to steer around them and still stay on the road.

Bracing every muscle and fibre in his body, he struggled to hold the powerful car straight. Another shot rang out from behind him. Briefly, in the mirror, he saw that the pursuing car was slowing automatically. They had come out of the bend more slowly than he had, evidently knowing of this obstruction. It was a trap of a sort, and he had driven into it. The offside wheels slammed into the rocks. Rubber shredded off the tyres as the needle-sharp edges tore into them. The car whirled viciously. Gritting his teeth, aware of the precipice that loomed on his right, he swung the wheel hard over. His control of the car lasted for only a split second. Then it went careening across the road in a dry skid, dust and rocks churning up beneath the wheels. His initial swerve had carried him clear of the lip of the precipice, choosing the rocks as the lesser of two evils.

Rearing savagely as it hit the pile of boulders, the car hung for several seconds, then crashed down onto its side, tearing along the boulder-strewn rock face, spinning round as it reached the end of the obstruction. The shuddering impact hurled Carradine from behind the wheel, knocking him with a sudden, savage force to one side. There was the splintering crash of glass, then the rending grind of metal being torn like paper. Moments later, the car came to a standstill against the rock face, the rear of it crumpled out of all recognition.

With a thin, high-pitched screech of brakes, the saloon drew to a halt beside the wreckage; but Carradine, slumped in the front seat, heard nothing of this. There was a thin trickle of blood on his left temple where his head had struck the dashboard. He was unconscious and almost immovable.

Opening the door, Minden climbed out and stretched his legs slowly, almost luxuriously, as if he had not a single care in the world. Then he walked slowly to the crumpled wreckage of the car and stood peering into the shattered window. He could just make out Carradine's body lying behind the wheel, his arms and legs twisted grotesquely where the front seat had torn away from its normal position.

Turning, he motioned to the two men in the car. 'Get him out of there,' he ordered harshly, 'and be careful. I want him alive.'

Nodding, the men went to work. One of them, a veritable giant of a man, gripped the twisted door that hung on smashed hinges in both hands and heaved, the muscles of his shoulders standing out beneath the cloth of the expensive, well-cut suit. Minden watched carefully. He was quite sure in his own mind that warped as they were, nothing short of a pull of almost half a ton would tear the door free of those hinges; yet slowly the metal was bending. Then with a shriek they snapped, the sudden release sending the other rocking back on his heels. He recovered his balance instantly, leapt forward and tossed the heavy door over the side of the precipice.

The other man squeezed himself into the small opening, ignoring the ragged slivers of twisted metal that tore at his suit. Reaching down, he pushed the seat back a couple of inches, just sufficient to withdraw Carradine's legs from beneath the dashboard. Then, sliding out of the car, he joined his companion and together they inched the inert, unconscious body clear of the metal.

Minden lifted the wrist and felt for the pulse. It beat irregularly and weakly against his fingertip. Nodding in satisfaction, he motioned to them to carry the other back to the waiting car. 'Be careful of him, but hurry. I don't want anyone else coming along this road until we're well away.'

'Where are we taking him?' asked the

thin man harshly.

'Back into town. Cornish's place is as good as any. Nobody will think of looking there. Besides,' he added with a vicious twist of his lips, 'he won't be there long enough for anybody to find him.'

The two men grinned as they thrust Carradine's body into the back seat of the car. One went back to the wreck where Minden waited impatiently, came running back with Carradine's Luger, handed it to Minden, then slid behind the wheel.

⋆ ⋆ ⋆

It was the lurch and sway of the car that eventually brought Carradine back to his senses; that, and the terrible aching agony in his body. He lay quite still, not opening his eyes, gritting his teeth together to prevent any sound from coming through his lips, which were stretched tight with the pain that lanced into his limbs.

Very slowly, memory returned to him. He recalled the car spinning out of control as the sharp rocks tore and chewed the rubber from the tyres; the

114

sudden lurch into the air as he hit the rock wall. After that, there was no memory at all. Mentally, he relaxed his limbs. As far as he could judge, no bones had been broken, although it was quite impossible for him to be sure of this without trying to move his arms and legs and feeling himself all over. There was a sharp stabbing pain that lanced through his chest each time he drew in a breath. His chest must have taken a hammering off the steering column of the car or the dashboard at the moment of impact. He could have cracked a couple of ribs, he thought tightly.

Still with his eyes closed, he listened to the muted roar of tyres on the road, felt the sway and jolt as they moved swiftly around sharp bends, and guessed that they were on their way back down the mountain road, heading towards Socorro. There was the feel of something hard but warm against his right leg, where it was twisted up on the seat of the car: one of the men seated next to him, maybe with a gun in his hand, ready to use it if he made one wrong move.

'Is he conscious yet, Marco?' asked a voice from the front of the car.

Carradine felt a sudden sharp blow in his side. It was only with a tremendous effort of will that he was able to stop himself from crying out loud with the agony of that skilfully delivered blow. Somehow he managed to lie still, letting all of the life go from his body so that it flopped limply against the back of the seat.

'Still out,' grunted a thick voice nearby.

'Keep an eye on him. This man is dangerous from all we know of him. Extremely dangerous.'

Carradine felt weak and impotent. Even though he was conscious, the bruising and battering which his body had received when the car had crashed had made it impossible for him to even put up any token resistance, even if he was able to take these men by surprise.

Very slowly, he opened his eyes to mere slits, not moving the rest of his body an inch. Now where would the men be? One driving. The other seated beside him, and the third man keeping an eye on him in the rear seat. Gradually, he was able to focus his vision on his surroundings. He could make out the smooth metal of the seat within an inch of his face, then the back of the front seat six inches away. The gleam of the metal ashtray set in it was just visible at the very edge of his vision if he twisted his eyes to their fullest extent.

With an effort, he tried to look along the length of his own body, to judge the position of the man seated near him. All he could see, however, was the tip of one brown shoe thrust out beneath the seat. Too far for him to do anything, even if he felt up to it. Besides, if there was a gun trained on him with an itchy trigger finger, then he would get a bullet in him for his pains, a split second after he made any move.

He lay still, breathing slowly and evenly, like an unconscious man might breathe. He needed time to think things out. His present position was precarious, but not hopeless so long as he remained alive. No doubt these men had searched him, although he doubted if they would have done it as thoroughly as they should in the short time that must have been available to them when they had dragged him out of that wrecked car. There were several very special weapons concealed about him, weapons constructed by the men in Division R back in London that even the American Secret Service probably knew nothing about.

There was the innocent watch on his left wrist for example. It told the time as any other watch, and the date changed automatically, but a couple of twists on the winder in the reverse direction and then a micrometric movement outward forced a slender metal needle from the centre of the face: a needle tipped with a very special type of drug, a curare-type poison, very similar to that used by the South American natives on their darts. If used in sufficient quantity, it could kill a man within seconds. This would paralyse the man within the same space of time once it was injected into the bloodstream.

There was the light, slender-bladed throwing knife that slid into a special pocket just inside the right-hand sleeve of his jacket. The gold cigarette case could squirt a nerve poison a distance of several feet, and it could be directed extremely accurately. At first, he had considered these weapons both bizarre and melodramatic. Now that he found himself in this predicament, he was glad he had them.

He realised that they were moving faster than before, and also that they had stopped the swerving, lurching motion that had evoked a feeling of sickness in the pit of his stomach. They had come down from the mountain road and were now driving along the main highway back into Socorro. And when they arrived there? What then? Would they take him into some dingy basement and try to beat the truth out of him? Would they use a drug on him to force him to tell them the truth as they had with that other poor devil who had set him on this trail?

Evidently their organisation was better equipped to discover things than he had given them credit for in the past. Cornish had moved fast to set these men after him so soon. They must have left Socorro within minutes of him, and they clearly knew who to follow. He tried to figure that one out. Just how had they known? How had Cornish been able to put them on to him so quickly? Mentally, he cursed himself for being such a stupid, blind fool as to think that these men would give him time before they acted. He had expected Cornish to make a move after what he had said to him that morning, but he had thought it would happen maybe two or three days later, once he had had time to get in touch with the men higher up in the Red Dragon and had received orders back from them.

Fifteen minutes or so passed. Then the car began to slow. He could hear the unmistakable sounds of the town traffic around them. There would be cars passing them every few seconds and people walking on the sidewalks, maybe within a few feet of the saloon — and no one suspected that he was lying there. It seemed incredible, and yet these men had been so clever that it was happening.

They turned a corner, slowed to a crawl, then moved on again with a smooth acceleration. The clipped tones from the front seat said: 'Go around to the rear of the building. No one will see it's there. Once we get inside, force him to walk upright. I don't care if it looks as if he's drunk, just so long as one of you keeps a gun in his back.'

There was a harsh, throaty laugh from the man seated beside Carradine. He said: 'This one of mine has a silencer on it. I'll keep it against the bottom of his spine. If there's any trouble, it'll blow his backbone apart and it'll just look as if he's fainted.'

The car slid to a stop. Carradine tensed himself. Should he make his move now, before they got him inside this building, wherever it was? It might be the only chance he got. He tried to shift his feet, to get them braced under his body, to give him plenty of leverage so that he might be able to hurl himself forward out of the car before any of these men could make a move.

Scarcely had the thought flashed through his mind than he felt fingers clutching around his arms, dragging him face downward along the car seat. Warm air hit his face as he was lifted from the car. He tried to move and uttered a low moan.

'He's coming round.'

'Keep a hold on him.'

The hard barrel of a gun was jammed into the small of his back. Flicking his eyes open, Carradine found himself staring at the broad, impassive face of the man standing near the car. It was a square, Teutonic face. His immediate reaction was that this was Minden.

Tightly, the other said: 'Don't try any wrong moves, my friend. We will not hesitate to kill you the instant you do.'

Carradine's voice was little more than a mumble as he said: 'Then why don't you?'

Unhurriedly, the other went on: 'Because there are some questions I should like to have answered. I have heard of you from various sources. They all say that you have a very high threshold of pain.' He smiled. 'However, there are some new techniques which may have been specially designed for people such as you. I think I can promise quite faithfully that when they are applied in your case, you will talk, and you will tell me the truth of what I want to know.'

'I can quite imagine the sort of things men such as you have dreamed up,' Carradine said. 'I suppose that you are Minden?'

'You are quite correct. I must confess that I had no idea my fame had travelled quite as far abroad.'

Carradine said tautly: 'You would be very much surprised to know just how much I know of you.'

'Perhaps.' Minden waved his hand airily. 'But enough of these pleasantries.' He motioned to the man standing behind Carradine. The front sight of the gun ground savagely into the other's back, just above the kidneys, and he stumbled forward, gritting his teeth as a red shaft of agony burned its way swiftly through the lower half of his body.

He was forced along the wide, winding drive. Lifting his head, he tried to push his sight through the blurring curtain of pain that shimmered in front of his vision. Only gradually was he aware of where they were. They were at the rear of the New Mexico Institute of Mining and Technology building.

5

Strange Ally

As he was urged along the drive that led to one of the doors at the back of the building, Carradine knew that Minden had some motive for bringing him here. There were bound to be people around in the corridors of the Institute — inquisitive people — yet the other showed no concern as the small party moved forward. Carradine suddenly made his decision.

The thin man opened the door, then paused for a long second in the opening, his back to them, his head turning slowly from side to side as he surveyed the corridor which lay beyond. At last, he made a quick movement with his left hand, gesturing them inside.

'Move,' grunted the man behind Carradine. The gun pressed a little harder into his back, emphasising the command.

Carradine took a couple of steps

forward, bringing him level with the thin man. Minden brought up the rear so that he was a short distance behind. With a wild, savage backward kick that struck the big man on the right knee, doubling him up with a harsh cry of agony, Carradine hurled himself forward. The throbbing ache at the back of his eyes increased in intensity as he made his move, but he had to ignore it. He had to keep moving. To stop now would be to give these men a chance to get on balance again.

He caught the thin man with his shoulder, knocking him sideways against the wall just inside the door. A thin whistle of pain gushed from the other's lips as he staggered. Out of the corner of his eye, Carradine saw him clawing for his gun, and brought the side of his right hand down hard on the man's wrist. With a yelp, the other fell back. There was no firm plan in Carradine's mind as he lunged forward. His only hope was to put as much distance between these men and himself as he could before they came after him, hoping that he might be able to mix with some of the crowd in the Institute

— making it difficult, if not impossible, for them to do anything. Whatever happened, he needed a little time to think out what to do.

Carradine had planned for the little man to fall, but he had not reckoned on the manner in which the other would go down. Whether or not the movement was deliberate, an out-thrust leg tripped him as he lurched forward, sent him skidding on the polished floor. Desperately, he tried to get his feet under him, to stay on balance. Behind him there was a sudden yell from Minden and the sound of the big man pushing his way inside.

Rolling over, twisting like a cat in mid-air, Carradine saw, through a pale haze, the big man rushing towards him. He kicked out blindly as the man reached him. His shoe connected with the other's thigh, bringing another grunt of pain from the thick, rubbery lips. Drawing back his leg, he aimed again at the knee, but this time the other was ready for him. Two hands flicked out, caught his ankle, and heaved violently, twisting at the same time. Pain jarred redly through his leg.

Sucking in a sharp breath, he tried to twist over onto his side as the other applied more relentless pressure.

His leg was being twisted all the way from ankle to thigh. He could make out the savage grin on the other's lips, the unholy light in the deep-set eyes. Soon, the other would pick him up and hurl him down again and it would all be over. Gritting his teeth, he hung on grimly. Sooner or later, someone must come along the corridor, even though it was at the rear of the building and therefore probably one of the least used.

As the other bent to obtain a better grip, Carradine's fingers scrabbled for a hold on the man's coat. The other shook him off with the ease of a terrier shaking off a rat. All of the breath was knocked from his body as the man slammed him back onto the hard floor. A clenched fist crashed into the side of his face. Head ringing from the force of the blow, Carradine tried to bring up his arm to block the second blow, but there seemed to be scarcely any strength left in his body.

Like lightning, moving quickly in spite

of his bulk, the other hit again just behind the ear, then kicked him with a savage violence in the small of the back. His skull cracked against the wall. Dimly, he heard Minden say sharply: 'That's enough. We don't want to damage him too much; not before he talks. Bring him along to the elevator. We'll have to carry him now.'

Slowly, Carradine felt himself slipping into the engulfing blackness of unconsciousness. Only vaguely did he know that arms gripped tightly, lifting him from the floor, holding him up with his feet dragging.

★　★　★

Harsh yellow sunlight streaming through his closed lids, glaring redly into his brain, brought Carradine slowly and painfully back to consciousness. He stirred feebly and tried to move. His arms moved slowly, sluggishly, as if they belonged to someone else, refusing to obey any conscious effort on his part. But his legs refused to move. He felt something warm trickling down his cheek. When it reached the corner of his mouth he tasted the saltiness of blood on his tongue.

Cautiously, he opened his eyes and stared dully about him. It was a large room, almost bare of furniture. There was not even a carpet on the floor. The criss-cross pattern of the wooden slats was clearly visible, with here and there a smear of white dust. The window through which the streaming sunlight fell on his face was dusty too, and he guessed that he was in some storeroom of the Institute. He felt the skin crawl on his body. He could guess what lay in wait for him here and he mentally cursed himself for his inexcusable folly in allowing this to happen. He had made an unforgivable — possibly even fatal — mistake in underestimating these men.

He realised that this was not the time for self-recrimination. He had to try to think of some way of getting out of this devilish mess. Letting his gaze slide sideways, he saw the man who stood a little behind him, leaning nonchalantly against the wall. It was a big man and Carradine derived a faint sense of pleasure at the

129

sight of the bloodied bruise on the side of the other's face and the manner in which he favoured one leg. Evidently his knee was still giving him a little trouble.

Gently, he tried to move his legs again, but found it impossible. There was a sharp pain around his ankles due to the cords tied tightly around them, binding his legs to the chair in which he sat.

The door opened. Glancing up, he saw Minden enter. Behind him, Cornish stepped through into the room. There was a look of sneering triumph on the latter's features. He walked over and stood in front of Carradine. Bending forward, he placed his hand under the other's chin, then jerked his head up and back. Lips twisted viciously, he said tightly: 'You have been extremely foolish, Mr. Carradine. Apparently you considered that your veiled threats against me would be sufficient for me to act foolishly. Instead, as must be apparent from your present position, it was you who were acting foolishly.' He stepped back, no expression now visible on his face. Very softly, he went on: 'Obviously you are working for the FBI, or one of the other departments. Consequently, there will be no need for us to pursue that point further. However, we do wish to know something. How much you know about us. Who your contacts are. Anything you may know of future moves against us.'

'If you think I intend to tell you anything about this, then your stupidity is greater than I gave you credit for,' Carradine said through tight lips.

Cornish smiled. 'There, my friend, you are quite wrong. We are serious men. Our business too is extremely serious. Your bodily health means absolutely nothing to us. When we have finished with you, you will be of no use whatever to anyone. We shall accordingly dispose of you by one of several methods open to us and there will be nothing whatever to point to us. So you see, it will be useless for you to resist us, as it will simply mean prolonging the agony for yourself.'

'Aren't you taking a bit of a gamble, hoping to torture me here?' Carradine asked. 'Surely there must have been dozens of other places, far more private, that would have suited your purpose far better.'

'Believe me, no one will think of looking for you here,' said Minden in precise, clipped tones.

'This storeroom is used exclusively by me,' Cornish explained. 'We shall be quite undisturbed. Besides, we know several methods of extracting the truth from a man. This should not take long. Then you will be removed and all trace of you will have vanished from this world. If they ever do find your body, I assure you that it will not be for a very long time, and by then it will be totally unrecognisable.'

'You seem to have thought of everything, haven't you?'

'Of course. We try to allow for every possibility. That is why, in the end, we shall destroy the West. Victory belongs to the strong, the utterly ruthless. That is why you will eventually be defeated, no matter what you do.'

'You seemed extremely unsure of yourself during our last meeting,' Carradine reminded him. 'Were you wondering what your bosses in the Red Dragon might do once they discover that it was a simple matter for us to locate you? Are you still wondering just how much we really know about you and how close we are to destroying you and your organisation?'

'If there is any slight doubt in my mind on that point,' murmured the other, 'then it will be put at rest within the next few minutes.'

The big man pushed himself away from the wall at a signal from Minden, and came forward with a singleness of design that sent a little tremor racing through Carradine's body. Cornish stepped back, regarding him contemplatively. Minden glanced curiously at Carradine for a moment as though expecting him to start talking, then nodded curtly.

'Begin,' he said harshly.

The big man stepped behind Carradine, where it was impossible for the other to see him. There was a faint movement behind the chair. An arm came into sight of the edge of Carradine's vision. There was the faint flicker of light on the bare knife blade. Then it moved down, slicing easily through the cloth of his sleeve without touching the flesh of his arm. Another quick motion and his sleeve fell away.

A pause, then the tip of the blade touched his cheek. There was a strangely cold bite of razor-sharp steel on skin. A thin scratch appeared from which blood began to well slowly, congealing in tiny, isolated drops. The pain was nothing compared to what had gone before, but it was the knowledge of what would continue that lifted the small hairs on the back of Carradine's neck and churned his stomach muscles into a hard, jangled knot.

Minden said something in a guttural tones. The knife was withdrawn swiftly. Speaking in English once more, he said: 'You still refuse to talk?'

'Yes.' Carradine spat the single word at him.

'Very well. We have plenty of time. Besides, we learn a lot from seeing how long a man can withstand a particular brand of torture. Interrogation is like everything else, subject to change according to circumstances.'

Carradine closed his eyes for a moment. The next second he was jerked sharply upright as the probing fingers of the man at his back squeezed into one of the nerve spots at the base of his neck. The pain that shot through him was so excruciating that for a fraction of a second it threatened to pass beyond the limit of human endurance. He almost blacked out with the sheer agony of it, but for him the blessing of unconsciousness failed to come. He remained aware of the pain as the other skilfully applied pressure to other points throughout his body, moving from one part to another with a practised hand.

It was obvious that this man knew his job far better than anyone else that Carradine had ever come up against. Desperately, he tried to breathe more slowly, forcing air out of his lungs each time he exhaled, hoping by this means to numb himself — to blur the endings of his nerves — but it had little effect on the pain.

'Stop.' Carradine scarcely heard himself say the word. Not until the awareness that the pain had ceased penetrated his numbed mind, did he realise that Minden had moved forward a couple of paces. The other's hand reached out, grasped him by the hair, and pulled his head back, staring down into Carradine's slitted eyes.

'Why prolong this agony, my friend?' he asked, in a faintly purring tone. 'All you have to do is answer some of our questions and it will all stop. Then you will be able to rest.'

'Go to hell,' Carradine muttered hoarsely. 'I'll tell you nothing.'

'Such a pity,' murmured the other. He released his hold so that the other's head slumped forward onto his chest once more.

There were more squeezings, more blows on his body. In the end, it seemed incredible that he would still be alive, let alone conscious throughout it all. His skull felt as if it were on the point of bursting. He tried to yell, to scream, anything to ease the pain that went on and on . . .

How long it continued, it was impossible to tell. Gradually, however, the accumulation of blows had its inevitable effect. The flickering darkness that had been hovering around the edges of his brain swept in. His head went forward onto his chest and this time, when the big man swung the straight edge of his stiffened hand against his back, there was no response.

Minden stepped forward, lifted the closed eyelids and peered down into still eyes. Then he felt professionally for the pulse in the left wrist. Letting Carradine's hand drop limply, he said shortly: 'He's lost consciousness. We can do nothing more until he comes round.' Glancing at the big man, he said: 'Stay here and keep an eye on him. We will resume the interrogation later.'

★   ★   ★

Very slowly, Carradine opened his eyes, then closed them almost at once as the sunlight half-blinded him, increasing the terrible pain that beat through his forehead. He moved his arms slowly. They were still free. His legs were tied, however. For a moment he waited, not moving, listening intently. He could hear nothing in the room. He opened his eyes and turned his head very slowly.

The round moon-face of the big man stared impassively at him. The other was seated in one of the other chairs, his legs thrust out straight in front of him, one hand resting in his lap. The thick fingers were wrapped around the butt of an automatic pistol.

Licking his lips, Carradine said harshly: 'You think I can have a drink of water?'

'I guess so.' The other eyed him wearily for a moment as if suspecting a trick, then went over to the small sink in one corner of the room, picked up a cracked tumbler, filled it with water and brought it over to him, keeping the pistol trained on him, his finger hard on the trigger. Carradine sipped the water slowly. It tasted of earth, but it eased the pain in his throat as it went down. He set the tumbler on the floor beside him. The thought of throwing it into the other's face had occurred to him, but with his legs tied to the chair, there would have been no chance at all of grabbing the gun.

'You may be able to kill me,' Carradine said, forcing himself to speak slowly and quietly. 'but that's as far as you will ever get. Minden is quite wise to be worried by how much I know, and what we're ready to do against you. We know all about the Red Dragon — who the members are, where they meet. I didn't come here alone. Every movement I've made has been traced and reported back to New York and Washington.'

'You're lying,' said the other flatly. 'They know so little about us that that can only be a small grain of the truth. Your secret service believes that because they arrest a few spies, they have justified their existence. If they only knew what is really happening under their very noses — '

'Suppose you tell me,' said Carradine sarcastically. 'We know all about Minden and Cornish. It was easy to find them both, and to tie them in with the theft of secret documents from the missile defence sites in New Mexico.'

'You know so very little. The Red Dragon is like an octopus. You may cut off the tip of one tentacle, but the rest the remains. And for America, indeed for the whole of the West, the time is running out very quickly. Naturally, we are interested in the missile sites in this area, but these are of only secondary importance. Shall we say a feint on our part.' The lips drew back in a grim smile.

Carradine started. Just what did the other mean by that? Was their main attack directed in some other direction? 'Aren't you afraid that by telling me all this, you may be jeopardising your entire efforts?'

'That would only be the case if there was any chance at all of you living to give any of this information to your colleagues. Unfortunately, as far as you're concerned, the chances of that are exactly nil.'

In the ensuing silence, Carradine heard the sound of footsteps approaching the closed door of the store room. The big man got smoothly to his feet and moved over to the door.

There came a sharp rap on the door. The big man turned the handle and opened it, still keeping his gaze on Carradine. There was a dull sound, no louder than a gloved fist striking a punchbag. For a long second after that, there was no other sound at all in the room. Then suddenly, for no apparent reason, the big man folded at the knees, then flopped forward onto his face into the room.

For a moment, Carradine stared stupidly at the man lying on the floor with his arms flung out, the shaft of sunlight streaming in through the curtainless window glinting off the smooth barrel of the pistol which lay a few inches this from his outstretched hand. It was almost as if his curled, clawing fingers were striving to reach it across the wooden floor.

Then a pair of slender legs came into sight, stepping delicately over the inert body. Slowly, scarcely able to believe his eyes, Carradine lifted his gaze and fought to focus it on the girl as she closed the door behind her. She came quickly towards him, going down on one knee as she wrestled with the knots of the cord binding his ankles.

'Candy!' he said, still scarcely comprehending. 'I don't know how on earth you got here, but thank God you came in time. What did you hit him with?'

'This,' said the girl. She picked up the length of heavy wood that lay on the floor beside her. 'It was the only thing I could find,' she said unashamedly. 'You don't think I hit him too hard?'

'Perhaps. But if you did it was something he deserved.' He got to his feet and felt the girl put an arm around him as he swayed; he would have fallen, but for her presence. The blood rushed pounding to his head, but he shook off the feeling with a savage, grim determination. At any moment now, the rest of these men might return. They had to get out of this place while they still had the chance.

Carradine had no idea how he was able to stay upright as he moved in the direction of the door. As he edged forward, his head swimming, his foot kicked against something hard. Staring down at it, he noticed the heavy automatic the big man had dropped. Bending, ignoring the sharp pain that jarred along the top of his skull, he picked it up, checked it expertly, then thrust it into the waistband of his trousers. At least he had a gun now. If they did run into those other characters there was a chance.

They made their way quickly along the corridor. Reaching the far end, Carradine turned to Candy. 'Do you know the layout of this place at all?'

'Yes,' she whispered back. 'I worked here for a couple of months during a semester. Just stick with me and we'll be outside in a couple of minutes.'

Carradine moved out into the wider corridor that opened up in front of them, then stopped, pushing the girl close against the wall behind him. A door had opened and three men stepped into sight. Recognition was immediate: Minden, Cornish and the thin man. They walked towards the pair in a loose bunch. Swiftly, Carradine looked about him. The nearest door was several yards away, too far for them to reach before the others came around the corner.

'We're cornered,' he hissed sharply. 'Stay behind me.'

'Don't worry,' she said softly. 'I know exactly what to do.'

'You're to stay out of range if there's any shooting,' he said tightly. 'These men won't stop at killing you.'

'I want *them* dead, all of them.'

In that instant, it came to him that

there was something far more than mere chance about her finding him so fortuitously. But there was no time to think about that now. The three men were less than ten feet away. As yet, they did not suspect the pair's presence just around the corner. Acting on impulse, Carradine twisted the winder of the watch on his wrists and pressed it slightly. There was a faint click, and then the slender needle was protruding from the watch-face like the sting of a wasp, but ten times as deadly.

Gripping the pistol tightly in his right hand, he stepped out into the corridor in full view of the men. The expression of surprise on Minden's and Cornish's faces was clearly visible. The thin man's face showed nothing and in that moment, Carradine had the inescapable feeling that he was the most dangerous of the three.

Hold it right there,' he said, the gun swinging smoothly in his hand to cover them all.

Minden said slowly, not once taking his eyes off Carradine: 'If you think that you will be able to get out of this building, then you're wrong. We are all armed and you won't be able to shoot the three of us before one of us gets you.'

'No? Then which of you wants to be the first to get a bullet?' He saw Cornish lick the corner of his mouth at that, and knew that in spite of the way in which he had spoken back in the store room, believing himself to be in complete control of the situation, the man was still a coward at heart. He would certainly not go for any hidden gun, even if he was carrying one. Carradine was not quite as sure about Minden.

He decided to take care of him first. With a quick gesture of the gun, he waved the German forward. Minden hesitated for a second, then stepped towards him, keeping his eyes fixed on the gun now, expecting to be either shot or clubbed with it. Carradine waited until the other was close enough, then swung his arm. But it was his left arm that moved, taking Minden completely by surprise. The watch caught him on the wrist. For a second, the other stared down in surprise at the tiny speck of blood that had formed on the small puncture. Then he lifted his head, looked up at Carradine and made to say something; but before he could force a word out, his face drooped slackly, the mouth falling open, the eyes turning up so that only the whites showed in the dim light. He dropped in a loose heap at Carradine's feet.

Before the limp body had hit the ground, the thin man made his move. He had evidently been waiting for something to momentarily distract Carradine's attention. The snub-nosed gun came up from the holster beneath his arm. And then it dropped, clattering to the floor, as the man went back, driven on to his heels by the impact of the slug in his chest. Swinging his glance back to Cornish, Carradine saw the astonished look of horror on the other's face, the stunned fear that blotted out every other emotion.

'Now turn around and walk out ahead of us,' Carradine ordered tersely. 'I don't know how many more of you there are wandering around on the loose in Socorro, but this time I'm taking no chances. Once

I've handed you over to the authorities I'll send them back for the others.'

★　★　★

'I've been looking into this remarkable statement of yours, Mr. Carradine,' said the Police Lieutenant quietly. 'I must admit that it sounds somewhat fantastic. After all, Albert Cornish is one of our most respected citizens. He has been working on occasion for the Government and I've heard nothing said against him.' He paused, frowning. 'However, I have sent a message through to the CIA in Washington. The reply should be back within half an hour. Until then, I suggest that you have a seat in the other office. I'll let you know the minute we get word from Washington.'

'Thank you.' Carradine nodded, glanced across at the girl, then got to his feet and went through into the other office, lowering himself gratefully into one of the chairs. His body felt like a mass of bruises, each contributing individually to the overall ache that was even worse than the pain he had experienced.

He glanced across at Candy, sitting demurely in the other chair. Taking out a cigarette, he lit it, blew smoke into the air, then said: 'Now perhaps you'll explain to me how you happened to be there just at the right moment.'

'You don't think it happened by chance?'

He shrugged. 'I might have thought that at first, but not after what you said when those three men started towards us.' He paused, eying her shrewdly. 'Just why did you want them killed?'

'I'm not sure what you mean.'

'No? The way I have it figured, you knew that Cornish was doing something crooked, even if you didn't know just what it was.'

For a moment, he thought she intended to deny it. Then: 'My father worked at one of the missile sites. He was driving home one night when another car forced him off the road. His briefcase containing secret documents was stolen and he was dead when he was eventually found the next morning. Cornish and Minden killed him. I know they did.'

'Then why didn't you go to the police

with this information? Let them handle it from there instead of trying to do it yourself?'

'Do you think they would have believed me? It would have been my word against Cornish's. You have just seen for yourself what they think of him. If the CIA in Washington don't come up with a good enough answer to that call, you'll discover for yourself just how well your word stands up against Cornish's. He's got a lot of standing and several very influential friends in Socorro.'

Carradine forced himself to relax. The girl's story made sense. He only hoped that the call which he had been allowed to make on his own account, through the coding section directed to Dean, would also start things moving from the New York end.

It was twenty minutes later when the Lieutenant came into the office. He gave Carradine and the girl a strange look, then said: 'Well, we just got the reply from Washington. Seems that your story checks out in every detail. They're sending a couple of men down for Cornish. In the meantime, we're to hold him here and see that nobody gets to him, not even his lawyer. This must sure be something really big.'

'Far bigger than you can possibly imagine,' Carradine told him wearily. He stood up. 'Will you be wanting us any longer?'

'No, you can go now.' The other nodded. He turned on his heel, then said: 'By the way, I have news for you from the Institute. My men found two men there. One was dead, shot through the chest. The other was in one of the store rooms at the back. He was unconscious. They have taken him to hospital. We'll question him when he comes round.'

'And the third man?' Carradine asked.

'There was no sign of him,' said the other apologetically. 'We found only the two. Either he recovered before my men arrived, or there was someone there who took him away.'

'I see.' Carradine bit his lower lip. So Minden was still free, out on the loose somewhere. It gave him a little shiver in the pit of his stomach.

6

Dew Line North

It was getting dark outside. Dean leaned forward in his chair and switched on the desk lamp in front of him. The ring of light threw his face into sharp relief. There were two thick files on the desk and he opened one of them, sitting and staring down at the first white sheet of paper for a long moment before speaking.

In the chair opposite him, Carradine crossed his legs and waited. This was the first time he had seen the other since he arrived back in New York almost three days earlier. During that time, he had spent his waking hours trying to discover as much as he could about the man called Minden. There had, unfortunately, been very little. The CIA seemed to have little on the other and it was evident that he had covered his tracks well and had worked undercover subtly and unobtrusively. Yet in all of the time he had been in the States, he must have been accumulating information, some from secret Government documents obtained by devious means from all over the country.

There had been several sensational spy cases during the past few years. Carradine had known some of them from first-hand knowledge where the ripples formed by the repercussions had flowed across the Atlantic to England. Yet in not one single incident had this man's name been brought out.

No wonder these men had been able to boast that the West had very little time before the Red Dragon struck in force. When that time came, the consequences were too terrible to contemplate. Clearly, China had bided her time well, staying out of the international limelight and leaving most of the spectacular successes to the Russians.

How little they really understood the Oriental mind. Ever since the days of Genghis Khan, these people had thought and acted with a different kind of patience to the people of the Western hemisphere. They could afford to allow generations to pass before they made their move. That was the real danger, the one they had to face up to now.

Dean looked up. 'The fact that Minden managed to slip through our fingers has altered things considerably, and made them far more difficult for us than they might otherwise have been,' he said softly. 'However, the fact that you would recognise him again is a help.'

Carradine placed the tips of his fingers together. He said: 'While I've been in New York, I've been thinking about the various details of this case, and something that the man who guarded me in the storeroom said has stuck in my mind.'

'Oh, what was that?'

'He said that the Red Dragon organisation is like an octopus. We could cut off the tip of one tentacle — meaning himself and Cornish with their hired killers — and still not damage the rest of the creature. He also said that the action down at Socorro was merely a feint.'

'You attached some importance to that remark?'

'Not at first. But the more I think about it, the more I'm inclined to believe that he really thought there was no chance of escape for me and he was telling the truth. Embellishing it a little, perhaps.'

'I suppose that you've made up your mind, what it's all about then.'

'Yes.' Carradine nodded. 'I've been doing a little research on my own, just filling in my time. It seems to me that if these people really wanted to put your defensive system out of action, then their target would not be down there in New Mexico, the furthest point from Redland. It will be much closer to the frontier than that.'

Dean grunted noncommittally. 'Go on,' he said very softly.

'Where is your top-secret front-line defensive system? Less than fifty miles from the Russian frontier, right on top of the world.'

'The Dew-Line system?'

'Exactly.' Carradine sounded definite. 'Of course not the early system you set up some years ago. The top-secret missile and listening post you've got in the Arctic.'

154

For a moment, the other allowed an expression of surprise to gust over his features. Then the impassive look returned. 'How in God's name did you learn about that?'

Carradine smiled at the other's momentary discomfiture. 'There are ways and means of getting information, particularly in my line of business,' he said easily. 'But seriously, doesn't it seem to you that this is where they must strike? The other bases you have are of only secondary importance compared with this one. And before you dismiss the possibility out of hand, just remember that we're dealing with an extremely well-organised group of men who will stop at nothing. We used to think that the Russian organisation was good, but believe me, they're nothing compared with the little lot that we've bumped up against now.'

'And if you are right in this assumption of yours — what would be your next move?'

'I'd like permission to go there,' Carradine said.

'To Station K?' This time the other was

unable to keep the surprise from his voice.

'That's right. Do you think you can swing it with them?'

Dean snorted. 'Surely you're not serious. All the men who we have there were checked and double-checked.' He tried to sound convincing.

Carradine persisted. 'I was asked to come here to help you. Perhaps some of my methods may seem a little unorthodox, but I've found in the past they usually get results.'

'Do you have any suspicions at all to go on? Apart from what this man said?'

'Yes, I have.' Carradine pointed to the smaller of the two files in front of the other. 'It's all in there if you care to read through it.'

'Suppose you give me the condensed version,' suggested Dean. Sitting back, he stared fixedly at Carradine.

Carradine grinned. There was just the possibility that the other had read all through that file during the previous night — Carradine had sent it through to him the day before — and knew every word of its contents.

'Very well. First of all, there was an accident with one of the snowcats. Fell into a crevasse, killing the three occupants. Two of the men were your agents and the third happened to be one of the top nuclear scientists at the station. That happened two years ago. Then there was the mysterious breakdown with one of the main reactors they have there for supplying heat and warmth for the station. It almost put them out of action completely and it certainly put back the operational date by six months. Lastly, two of the main stores containing electronic equipment were destroyed by a fire which broke out under circumstances which have not yet been satisfactorily explained.'

'You appear to have done your homework extremely well and conscientiously. I must admit that when these events are taken together, there does appear to be a case against coincidence.'

'Then you will pull a few strings?'

Dean was silent for a long moment. 'I'll do what I can. This may take a few days.'

'We may not have that long,' Carradine said seriously. He could feel a little of the tension balling up inside him as he got to his feet, the interview at an end.

★ ★ ★

The plane droned high above the brown and green earth some fifteen thousand feet below them. To the north, Carradine could just make out the tall, rearing peaks of the range of mountains ahead of them. There was the smooth, flat whiteness of snow, glaring in the sunlight that flooded the ground. He sat in the bucket seat of the Air Force plane and watched the snow-covered ground inch closer to them. In spite of their air speed, they were so high, and the ground here stretched so far away in an almost endless sea of brown, green and white, that even minutes of flying seemed to make no visible impression on the distances concerned.

'Coffee, sir?' inquired the voice at his elbow.

Carradine turned. The young Air Force sergeant held the tray out to him. There was a mug of steaming coffee on it and a small plate of biscuits.

'Thanks, I could certainly use this.' He accepted the tray gratefully, balancing it on his knee. Sipping the scalding coffee, he said: 'How long before we arrive at our destination?'

The sergeant glanced at his watch. 'Another forty minutes. We were delayed a little when we had to skirt around an electrical storm. When you're as far north as this, anything like that can play hell with the magnetic compass. Apart from the effect it could have on the plane itself. We usually try to avoid these storms if at all possible.'

'Why couldn't we fly direct to Station K?' Carradine asked.

'Afraid that isn't possible. There's a plane twice a week making this trip from the forward base. They'll get you a seat on it. We just do the routine run out to Alaska.'

'I understand.' Carradine settled himself deeper in his seat, striving to discover a position that would give some comfort to his long, angular body. Obviously the seats had not been designed with the comfort of the passenger in mind.

The sergeant went back into the cabin. Carradine caught a glimpse of the pilot seated behind the controls, earphones clamped on his head. Then the curtain dropped back and he was alone once more with the monotonous drone of the powerful engines in his ears to keep him company and the thin, high-pitched keening of the wind around the fuselage. Down below, they had left the tundra behind them and there was only snow with an occasional patch of brown to break the monotony. A bleak and strangely forbidding country, he reflected as he finished the coffee and chewed on the biscuits. Yet no doubt it was much to be preferred to the north where Station K was situated. He had gathered a few details of the station from the files in New York.

Evidently virtually all the base was under the ice, with only a small handful of wooden huts on the surface. The complement of the place was over five hundred men when it was fully manned, but at the moment there were less than two hundred there, most of them scientists and military personnel. Atomic reactors provided them with most of the essential comforts of home. There was no doubt that it had been a tremendous feat of military engineering and that it would be one of the first targets for an organisation such as the Red Dragon. Yet there was still the nagging little thought at the edge of his mind that he may, after all, have made a mistake and those three disturbing incidents had been nothing more than the long arm of coincidence.

He closed his eyes and tried to relax. The odd mixture of smells that seemed always to be present inside a military plane which were never there in one of the large luxury airliners, assailed his nostrils, making him feel a trifle queasy in the pit of his stomach.

The minutes passed with an agonising slowness as far as Carradine was concerned. Then, off in the distance, he made out the cluster of buildings, standing out starkly against the background. For a moment, the plane seemed to be turning away from them, heading off in a totally different direction. Then he noticed the runway about a quarter of a mile from the buildings and at almost the same instant, the plane came in on its downward glide, swinging slowly to align itself with the runway.

There was a prickling, unpleasant sensation in Carradine's ears as they lost height. The undercarriage locked itself into place with a faint jar. Then the ground was rushing up to meet them. He closed his eyes instinctively for a second as the snow seemed ready to engulf them, to reach up and snatch at the belly of the plane, dragging it down totally out of control. There was a vague glimpse of a rutted road leading away from the runway in the direction of the huts, and of a telephone wire strung between tall poles. Then they were down and there was a soft, scarcely perceptible thump as they landed. Carradine led his breath go in a long, audible sigh.

The curtain was raised and the sergeant came through, a cheerful grin on his face. 'I'll take you over to the base,' he said. 'They'll find you a bed for the night and something to eat.'

'You know when the plane for Station K leaves?'

'Some time tomorrow, I think,' said the other. 'The Major will be able to tell you.'

Carradine felt the icy blast of air hit him the instant he stepped down from the plane and followed the sergeant over to the collection of long, wooden huts. It had been warm inside the plane. Now perspiration condensed swiftly on his body, his shirt clinging damply to his back.

There was hot coffee waiting for them inside the small control room. The tall man seated near the window got to his feet as they entered and came forward, hand outstretched.

'You'll be Commander Carradine,' he said genially. 'I'm Major Allison. I heard you were to arrive over the radio a couple of hours ago. Understand you'll be flying on to Station K tomorrow.'

'That's right.' Carradine nodded. He held out his hands towards a stove in the middle of the room. 'Tell me, is it as cold as this up there at the forward station?'

'Even worse,' said the other with a broad grin. He filled a mug of steaming

163

coffee and handed it to Carradine. 'Better wrap yourself around this. It'll bring a little of the feeling back into you. We live on the damned stuff here. That, and the Scotch which comes in on most of the flights.' He nodded his head towards the window and, glancing out, Carradine was just in time to see half a dozen heavy crates being carried into one of the adjoining huts. He had noticed them when he had been on board the plane and had wondered about them. Now he knew exactly what they were.

'You seem to have most of the comforts of home here,' he observed.

'Most of them,' agreed the other. 'The isolation is the worst part as far as the men are concerned. They usually do a one-year term out here before going back home.' He paused, waiting until Carradine had drained the coffee, then went on, giving him a shrewd glance. 'I don't suppose you can tell me why you want to get up to Station K? It's usually strictly out of bounds except for very exceptional personnel.'

'I can understand that.' Carradine nodded. 'I'm afraid I can tell you very little. I'm simply going there to take a look around the place. From what I've heard it's the last word in an early warning system and apart from being a defensive base, it can also be put on an offensive footing in a matter of minutes.'

'So I've heard,' said the other dryly. 'As for me, I'm glad I'm here and not up there.' He spoke without a flicker of change in his expression. Evidently the Major knew how to play it cool.

'My only concern at the moment is getting there. I had a little difficulty getting the right strings pulled to get me as far as this.'

'I think we can promise to get you there on time tomorrow afternoon,' said Allison quietly. 'At least we don't have to worry overmuch about other planes using the routes in that direction. There are occasions, of course, when severe electrical storms or blizzards can clamp down on everything, and when that happens we simply have to sit tight and wait until things calm down again before making a move. Here, near the North Pole, we're more at the mercy of nature than anywhere else on Earth.'

'I hope nothing like that turns up tomorrow.'

'Shouldn't think so.' The other shrugged. 'The weather seems to be pretty stable at the moment. Anti-cyclonic. Can't guarantee what it will be like nearer the pole, of course. But this is the wrong time of the year for the really bad stuff to hit us.' He moved away from the window. 'I have to discuss one or two things with the Exec Officer, Commander, if you'll excuse me. Sergeant Grenson will show you to your quarters. Dinner is at eight-thirty tonight.'

'Thanks, Major.' Carradine followed Grenson out of the hut.

* * *

When Carradine woke the next morning he was still heavy with sleep — the utter heaviness of a man who has slept for a long time. Throwing back the thick covers on the bed, he glanced at the luminous dial of the watch on the small table. It said eight-fifteen. Outside it was still dark, with only a few lights to be seen in the direction of the landing strip and the control block. The shape of two military transport planes could just be seen on the narrow perimeter track.

Swinging his legs to the floor, he washed, shaved, then went out into the main dining hall. Two men were seated at one of the tables; they had evidently been on duty all night.

'Is it always dark here at this time of the morning?' Carradine asked.

The taller man grinned. 'We're heading into the winter, sir. Pretty soon, we'll be shut in all the time.'

'Then I'm glad my stay here won't be too long a duration.'

'You're heading up north to Station K, aren't you?' queried the other man.

'That's right. Conditions there will be even worse than here, I suppose.' Carradine sat down in the empty chair at the table and a few moments later, a white-coated steward came over, took his order and vanished into the room at the back of the wide mess.

'I wouldn't say that exactly,' countered the tall man. 'Chuck here and I take the plane up there once a week. Things can be pretty awful at times, but once you're inside the base itself, you've got all the luxuries and comforts of home. Believe me, you've seen nothing like it. They've got a whole goddamn city up there under the ice.'

'I can't wait to get there and see it all for myself,' Carradine said as his breakfast was placed in front of him.

Chuck gave a shrewd stare as he commenced eating. 'Forgive me saying this. But it seems to me that you must be on some really important mission to even get permission to go there. I take it that you're not a military man?'

Carradine nodded. 'A friend of mine managed to pull a few strings in the right quarters and here I am.'

Chuck shook his head. 'I don't know how you wangled that. Still, Darren and I will be glad of your company on the flight this afternoon. The Met boys reckon that we should have a smooth and uneventful flight. Trouble is, I never take what they say as gospel. I always find that something turns up on the route to give us a bumpy journey. Especially at this time of the year.'

'You wouldn't be trying to spoil my appetite for this excellent breakfast, would you?' said Carradine, grinning.

'Sorry.' The other shook his head. 'Wasn't thinking, I guess. We spent most of the night checking the plane. Everything seems OK.' He glanced at his watch, then scraped back his chair. 'Now if you'll excuse us, we'll grab ourselves a little shut-eye before this afternoon.'

Carradine watched them leave, then settled himself in his chair and finished his breakfast, washing down the excellently cooked food with hot, sweet coffee. He had just finished and was sitting back, when a voice behind him said genially: 'Good morning, Commander. Sleep well?'

'Close on ten hours, Major.' Carradine motioned to one of the empty chairs. 'Breakfasted even better. You know how to look after yourselves here.'

Allison smiled. 'It's the only thing we have to do to make life bearable. We're right at the very edge of civilisation here. Sometimes, I think it may be better for us if we were a hundred miles or so to the north. At least then we wouldn't be in this limbo; we'd be clear into Hell. When you know that you're such a long way from civilisation, you can acclimatise yourself to the loneliness a little more quickly.'

It was a moot point of psychology, Carradine thought; but maybe the other had got something there. 'I've just had breakfast with the two men who will be flying me out this afternoon,' he said, changing the subject adroitly.

Alison nodded briefly. 'They're both good men. Veterans of the Korean War. And they can handle the planes in this weather as well as you or I could drive a car through New York. I'll get you some protective clothing, though, before you leave. Although you may not need it once you're inside the base itself, you have quite a way to go from the landing strip and there's a blizzard blowing there almost all the time, so it's best to be prepared for everything.'

'Thanks again for all you're doing.'

'Not at all. My orders were very explicit: to give you all the help I can. It isn't often that we get anyone like you out here. I can guess that there is something big involved.'

'Perhaps, but believe me, the less you know about it, the better.'

'So I've gathered,' murmured the other enigmatically. 'I hope you won't take this to heart, but shortly after you arrived here, I put an urgent call through to New York. You must admit that there seems to be something odd about this entire venture — a civilian coming along, given virtually a *carte blanche* to do as he likes, to be afforded every facility.'

'And what sort of reply did you get back, Major?' asked Carradine, lifting his brows slightly.

'Simply that your credentials were beyond question. That you are acting on the highest authority. I can't go against anything like that, now, can I?'

'I certainly hope not,' said Carradine fervently. 'I'd go to any lengths to carry through this mission.'

'Don't worry. We'll see to it that you arrive safely at Station K. What happens after that is out of our hands.' There was a curious look on his face and he seemed to have added the last statement as an afterthought.

Carradine guessed at the reason behind it. 'So you've heard of some of the odd happenings there too?'

Allison nodded. 'Too many things to be explained away by coincidence. But so far, no one back in Washington or New York seems to have taken any notice of this.'

'Well they have now,' Carradine said tightly.

★   ★   ★

The plane was an old Douglas DC-3 Dakota, old but particularly well suited to the task of ferrying men and supplies across the blizzard-strewn Arctic wastes. The two propellers turned slowly as the engine coughed, then spewed out several puffs of black smoke. Within moments they had become whirring pools, and the scream of the engines rose to an ear-splitting whine that grated on Carradine's nerves as he sat on the low step immediately behind the pilot. Vibration tore at the fuselage of the plane as it began to roll along the perimeter track, moving in the direction of the landing strip.

'You all right back there?' asked Chuck, turning his head.

Carradine could just make out the words above the roar of the engines. He gave the thumbs-up sign to indicate that all was well.

The Dakota jerked abruptly as Darren released the brakes. There was a pale green flare hanging low over the control building in the distance. Then they were racing along the runway, screaming with a banshee wail over the windsock at the far end, a windsock that stretched out to its furthermost limit by the wind which had got up during the past hour or so. The plane lifted more slowly than Carradine was accustomed to and he had to tell himself that this was no modern airliner he was in, and that the equipment and supplies which had been stacked neatly at the back must weigh several tons, dragging down the plane.

Over the end of the runway, they circled, then headed north-east, out to where the endless wilderness of ice and snow lay in front of them, stretching away to the far horizon. He felt a little shiver go through him as he let his gaze wander over the rough ground where tall, clawing peaks lifted to the greying sky. The sun lay somewhere behind them, but there seemed to be a haze clouding it a little and they did not seem to be able to climb above it.

For an hour, they flew over a terrain that was completely featureless but for the mountains that jutted up now and again directly in their path. They were flying at close on ten thousand feet, he reckoned; but even so, several of these peaks were almost on a level with them as they flew steadily northward.

Turning in his seat, Chuck waved an expressive hand in the direction of the flight-covered ridges that seemed to reach up and claw for the belly of the plane as if striving to pull them down from the unfriendly skies. 'Don't let these bother you,' he called loudly. 'When you've flown this route as long as we have, you find that these mountains are the least of your worries, unless you happen to run into a particularly dense blizzard when your visibility is so low that you're in danger of running into them.'

'At least there should be no danger of that today.' Carradine said, hoping that his tone sounded a little more full of conviction than he was himself. Many of the peaks outside seemed to be eternally shrouded in mist, looming up out of the writhing haze, then vanishing again behind them.

'It isn't too bad at all,' confirmed the other. He glanced down at the map spread out on a pad on his knee and then rifled through the papers firmly clipped to it. 'Pressure seems to be dropping a little, though, to the north. We may run into dirty weather there. Fortunately, by that time we ought to have cleared the mountains.'

Carradine nodded and peered down through the small window near his head. Down below, there was an endless sea of white, dazzling to the eye even with only dim sunlight flooding it. Lifting his gaze, he stared over Chuck's shoulder. There was something more than a dim haziness on the horizon in front of them now; something thicker, and more definite — more dangerous. He touched the co-pilot on the shoulder. Pointing through the cockpit, he said in a harsh tone: 'What's that up ahead, Chuck? Trouble?'

The other stared out into the white distance for a moment, and then gave a brief nod. 'Very likely it is,' he said flatly. 'Like I said back at the airstrip, I never believe a word these Met men tell me. Looks as if I was right again. Whenever we get a low pressure area in this part of the north it means snow, perhaps even an electric storm.'

'Can't you fly around it?'

'That may not be as easy as it sounds. They can move pretty quickly and erratically. That means we'd find it virtually impossible to predict its movement over the next hour or so. Our best bet is to head straight for it as Darren is doing now. Could be that we'll only run through the trailing fringe of it if we're lucky. If not then we'll be flying blind for an hour or so.'

'Can't you radio station K and get a weather check from them?'

'Sure, we could do that. But if that is

an electrical storm out there our signals won't have much chance of getting through.' As if to prove this, he leaned forward and switched on the radio. The crackle and hiss of static boiled in Carradine's ears and he nodded in answer to the lift of Chuck's eyebrows.

'I see what you mean,' he called loudly. Inwardly, he felt the sensation of danger. Many times in the past, this feeling of premonition had come to him; it was something he could never explain satisfactorily to himself.

The Dakota dropped with a sickening sensation as they hit an air pocket. In spite of the tight grip he had on himself, Carradine grasped the metal stanchion nearby, his fingers curling around it and biting into the palm of his hand.

Just how many flying hours had this DC-3 done? he wondered tensely. Sooner or later, metal fatigue ate its way into the structure and it needed only the kind of battering it got flying through a storm such as this for its strength to give way. In addition to this, the extremely low temperature also had an inevitable effect on metal. He tried not to think of this as they dropped again. His stomach lurched up into the place where his chest was supposed to be.

Glancing around out of his half-shut eyes, he saw Darren fighting with the controls. A vivid blue flash glanced across the edge of his vision and the plane rocked and swayed like a mad thing, as if a giant invisible fist had suddenly, and without warning, smashed against the fuselage, hurling the plane like a stone across the berserk heavens. There was no sign whatever of the sun. All that could be seen in the strange murky gloom outside were the white, whirling clouds of snow as the storm closed in on them from all sides.

Chuck grinned down at him. 'Looks as though your first trip has turned out to be a real lulu,' he said, pressing his lips close to Carradine's ear. 'Not often we hit it as bad as this.'

'How long before we get through it?'

'Hard to say. We could come out of it in a few minutes, or it could go on for an hour or so. All we can do now is sit tight and hope that the lightning misses us.'

Carradine suddenly realised how frail and helpless the plane really was; how puny mankind was when it came to facing up to Nature in the raw like this. There were forces at work here which men would never be able to tame. Desperately, he struggled to close his mind to what was going on all around him — to shut out the sound of the storm and the tremendous blue-white flashes of lightning as they zigzagged across the sky.

At length, however, after many minutes of agonising uncertainty, the sky gradually began to lighten around them. The vivid thunderclaps faded into the distance. At first, it was impossible for him to believe that they were actually flying out of it, that they were airborne and nothing drastic had happened to them.

The roar of the engines seemed to settle down to a steady whine. With an effort, Carradine turned his head and glanced through the window. He caught brief glimpses of the ground through what seemed to be a swirling fog, but which he knew to be the blizzard raging around them. Then, at length, the storm drew away from them, and the air cleared as if by magic. He saw that they were flying over large ice floes, most of them packed closely together so that apart from very faint, scarcely seen cracks, they appeared to be part of one massive block of ice floating majestically in the serenity of the Arctic Ocean.

Chuck let out his breath in a faint whistle and glanced along the rows of instruments in front of him. 'Guess we made it all in one piece,' he said softly. He checked on the figures he had been scribbling on the pad in front of him. 'In spite of the delay, I figure that our time of arrival should be only fifteen minutes or so late. Another fifty minutes.'

'I can't wait for it,' Carradine said with earnest feeling. He sat back in the chair and waited as the minutes ground themselves past.

Chuck touched him on the arm and pointed down through the cockpit. 'Take your first look at station K.' There was an odd note in his voice.

Carradine looked. At first, he could

make out nothing. The ice and snow stretched as far as the eye could see. Then, following the direction of Chuck's pointing finger, he could just make out the small cluster of huts standing out blackly on the snow. 'Surely that can't be it?' he said, scarcely believing what he saw.

'That's it,' Chuck grinned broadly. 'And that's all the Reds would see from the air if they sent any of their spy planes over for a quick look. Nothing to mark it out from a small weather station.'

'I agree.' Carradine nodded. The Dakota swung around in a wide, descending circle and he was able to make out the long landing strip within half a mile of the huts. Then he saw something else. Now that they had reached a sufficiently low altitude, he was able to pick up the faint tracery of tracks in the snow, leading up to one point and then stopping for no noticeable reason. Not until his eyes suddenly adjusted to the perspective was he able to see that they vanished simply because at that point there was a steep decline in the ice; that a vast tunnel had been hollowed out of the ice and snow, leading down to a point several hundred feet below the surface.

Almost all of Station K was two or three hundred feet beneath the solid, unyielding surface of the ice.

7

City Under the Ice

Stepping out of the plane, Carradine felt a cold more intense and numbing than anything he had ever previously experienced. Ice crackled a little under his polar boots and the biting wind tore through the thick furs of his clothing and lifted small shards of ice, driving them at him, slashing across the exposed flesh of his face until it seemed to be torn to ribbons. He lowered his head instinctively and waited for Chuck and Darren to climb down.

Stamping his feet, he flailed his arms to keep the blood circulating through his body, shivering continually. Within a couple of minutes the ice and snow, whipped off the crests of fantastically shaped white dunes like some glaring, bleached Sahara, had brought a numbness to his flesh so that he could feel nothing. Whenever the wind died for a moment, the rustling of the slivers of ice as they slid forward over the smooth surface was like a horde of insects on the march.

Slapping his gloved fists together, Chuck dropped lightly to the ground, adjusted his goggles, and said: 'Better keep your head down. This flying ice can give you a nasty cut in no time at all.'

Darren rubbed the fog from his goggles and peered about him. 'No sign of that goddamned jeep,' he observed. 'I suppose that they expect us to walk again.'

Chuck said: 'This is becoming a long-standing grudge between the men here and ourselves. They're supposed to send a jeep or a small snowcat out for us, to take us down into the station, but quite often it slips their minds and we have to walk it.'

'Guess we'd better get started then,' Carradine muttered, the bitter wind snatching the words from his mouth and whirling them away. Bending forward into the teeth of the wind, he forced his legs to move. He had not guessed how difficult it was to walk on this stuff. At one moment he would be slipping and sliding helplessly in all directions and at another, the upthrusting spikes of ice would make movement almost impossible. Chuck and Darren moved alongside him, their furs swiftly becoming white as the powdery snow was lifted from the ground and hurled at them.

There was a high ridge blocking their path a few minutes later. Carradine, moving up just behind the other two, came on it with a sense of surprise. How in God's name could there be a ridge there when everything had looked to be so perfectly flat between the plane and the small cluster of wooden huts? Then it came to him that in this utterly white wilderness, it was virtually impossible to have any sense of depth at all when looking out across the terrain.

He stumbled forward after the others, mentally cursing the men at the station for not sending that transport out to meet them. Most of the way they stuck close to the ridge so that it shielded them from the full, biting fury of the wind. Here, it was possible to straighten their backs a little, to lift their heads and look about them through the protective goggles.

They hit the end of the ridge so abruptly that the sudden change from calm to a gale-force wind took them off-balance. Carradine was almost bowled off his feet. Only by reaching out instinctively and catching hold of Chuck's coat was he able to stay upright.

In spite of the wind, the going seemed easier now. They were no longer struggling uphill. They had hit the downgrade and were now less than a quarter of a mile distant. Off to the left, Carradine could now plainly see the entrance to the great shaft, which led down beneath the polar ice to Station K. It looked massive — a tremendous construction. How anyone had the engineering ability to construct such a place out here in the depths of the Arctic was momentarily beyond him.

He mentioned this to Chuck. The other grinned and wiped some of the snow from his collar. 'If you think that's something, then wait until you see what they have down below. That will take your breath away and — ' He broke off sharply, suddenly. The sharp crack of a rifle sounded, briefly but unmistakable, on the thin air. In the same instant, Carradine felt the wind of the slug pass his face, less than a couple of inches from where he stood.

'Hey! There's some goddamned idiot shooting at us from one of the huts,' exclaimed Darren. 'What the hell do they think they're trying to do?'

'Maybe they got us tagged for a trio of polar bears,' suggested Chuck. He was grinning faintly, but the smile was oddly strained. He lifted his arms and waved them emphatically. There was no sign of movement among the huts. Yet it had been from that direction that the gun had been fired.

'I reckon we'd better get in there before whoever it is decides to take another shot at us and makes a better job of it the next time,' Carradine said. Inwardly, he had the feeling that the bullet had been intended for him. It made little sense. If that was the case, then it would be only explainable on the assumption that there was at least one person here who knew his identity and why he was here.

It seemed impossible that Minden could have got away and given the alarm. The other did not know that he was coming out here. But he could think of no other explanation.

They moved across a smooth patch of ice and reached the nearest hut some ten minutes later. It was empty, but going on to the next they found three men manhandling large oil drums from one side to the other.

'Any of you three men been outside in the last fifteen minutes?' Chuck yelled.

The men turned, then shook their heads. One of them, with a sergeant's chevrons on his sleeve, stepped forward. 'Nobody's been outside here,' he said. His gaze switched to Carradine and for a moment there was a look of perplexity on his face. Then the inscrutable expression returned.

'Anybody else here?' Darren asked.

Again the other shook his head. 'Lieutenant Venders was here half an hour ago, but he went back to the station.'

Darren looked around at Carradine. 'You want to take a look through the other huts?'

Carradine considered that, then shook his head slowly. 'I doubt if it would show us anything. Whoever it was fired that shot, he will be down in the station by now. He must've spotted us coming over the snow some distance away and when that first shot missed, rather than have another try, he slipped away so as not to be discovered.'

'A shot?' The look of amazement on the sergeant's face was quite obviously genuine. 'When was this?'

'About a quarter of an hour ago,' Carradine said. 'Somebody fired a shot at us as we were coming in. Maybe it was a mistake. They could have thought we were something else.'

Chuck said harshly: 'Until we discover something, I'd be glad if you and your men here keep this little incident under your hats. We don't want it to be blown up into something out of all proportion to what it really is. No sense in getting everyone steamed up for nothing.'

189

'We understand perfectly, sir.'

They made their way slowly between the rows of huts. As far as Carradine could see, they were all deserted. Not until they were approaching the entrance to the tunnel leading down into the main base was there any sign of movement, or any sound. The snowcat came rumbling up from the depths, treads sliding a little in the smooth hard-packed snow. Slowly, it nosed its way up into the open and Carradine was able to make out the man in the totally enclosed cabin, operating the controls.

The snowcat drew level with them, then stopped. The cabin opened as part of it slid to one side.

'Howdy,' said the man in the high seat. 'Sorry I didn't get over to meet you at the plane. Had a little trouble with the controls. First time it's happened with this particular machine. Usually we have no bother with it.'

'What sort of trouble?' Chuck asked as they climbed inside.

'Electrical,' said the other tersely. 'Can't understand it myself. It was working perfectly this morning when I checked everything through.'

Carradine lifted his brows a little. 'You think it may have been tampered with since you looked at it?'

The man turned to stare at him closely for a moment, then looked around at Chuck. 'Who is this?' he asked. 'I was told there would be three coming in, but they said nothing about who the civilian was.'

Chuck grinned. 'I reckon it's all right to talk in front of the Commander,' he said quietly. 'He's been given clearance all the way from the top.'

'I see.' It was evident from the other's expression that he did not see at all, but he was not going to admit that. He turned the snowcat adroitly and they moved slowly back into the looming tunnel in the ice. 'Well,' he muttered at length, 'if you want my opinion, then it could have been tampered with. There have been some funny things happen here while I've been on the station. Things that nobody has explained.'

'And have they been reported?' asked Carradine.

'Oh, sure, they have to be reported. You can't hide murder for very long.' There was a note of bitterness in the man's tone, which Carradine spotted at once. He stared at the other for long seconds, then swung his gaze back to the front, peering through the transparent plexiglas of the observation dome of the snowcat. They were halfway down the smooth incline now, moving into the deep shadow cast by the rising wall of ice. But down below, there seemed to be plenty of light; it flooded into the tunnel from the walls where they closed in overhead, and lit the gleaming rails that ran the entire length of the tunnel, deep into the interior of the ice cap. Carradine felt lost in the wonder of it all, in a partial comprehension of the tremendous feat of engineering that he was witnessing every second that the snowcat ground its way forward. Then they were deep in the heart of the ice. For a moment the feeling of claustrophobia was almost unbearable. Then he had succeeded in shrugging it off and in its place there was a sense of wonder back again. Somewhere in the distance there was a soft, steady thudding of machinery, of giant turbines supplying the power to this tremendous hive beneath the Arctic snow.

'My orders are to take you straight to the Colonel,' said the driver, glancing obliquely at Carradine. 'Chuck and Darren will go to their usual quarters.'

'We'll be taking the plane back tomorrow,' Darren explained. 'With the DC-3 there's no chance at all of making the round trip in the one day. We have to stop over for the night.'

* * *

Colonel Brinson was a tall man. Carradine guessed that he was not far off six-foot-six and his grip was enough to make him wince as the other shook hands and then motioned him to a chair in the spacious, well-furnished office. For a moment, Carradine imagined that he must be somewhere back in America, that this place could surely not exist under those countless thousand tons of solid ice and snow. With an effort, he brought himself back to the present.

Brinson sat back in his own chair and regarded him closely for ten seconds before speaking. 'That door, and the walls of this office, are as near soundproof as it's possible to make them. You can speak quite freely here.'

'Thank you,' Carradine said. 'I am not sure how much you already know about this sordid business.'

'Very little, I assure you. Not that I haven't suspected something for a very long time now. First the accident in the crevasse, then the fires. They all began to add up to something far more sinister than coincidence.'

Carradine nodded slowly. 'These — incidents, as you call them — they haven't stopped. As we were making our way here, somebody hidden in one of the supply huts on the surface took a pot shot at me. Had the bullet been an inch or two to the right it would have been the end as far as I'm concerned.'

Brinson's face tightened just a shade. 'You're sure that they were trying to kill you? It could have been an accident or a mistake. Several of my officers carry weapons and go hunting on the ice.'

'I had considered that, but it was what the driver of the snowcat told me that convinced me that it was an attempted murder. He said that the electrical system developed a fault just as he was on his way to pick us up. But he had it checked thoroughly only a little while before and everything had been working perfectly. Evidently someone sabotaged the snowcat so that I would have to walk from the plane and thereby present them with an excellent target.'

'God, what an unholy mess.' The other leaned forward on the table. 'Where is it going to end? And what's just as important, who's behind it all — the Russians?'

'Not this time.' Carradine shook his head slowly, then went on to briefly outline the known facts, beginning with the murder of Sen Yi in London and the smashing of the small Red Dragon cell in Socorro. The other said nothing until he had finished; but as the minutes passed, his face grew tighter and more sombre.

'No wonder that Washington are worried. If they manage to destroy the station, it would mean that we would lose our means of detecting any missile launchings in the Soviet Union, or China too for that matter, within a minute or so of them getting off the launching pad.'

'You can do that now?' Carradine asked.

Brinson nodded. 'You'd really be surprised at the number of top-flight scientists we have stationed here, and also the full range of electronic equipment. There are three atomic reactors down here, which supply us with all of the energy we need. We could stay here indefinitely, almost, even if we were cut off from the outside world.'

'Just how far are you from the Russian frontier?'

'Just step across the ice, take a short boat trip and you could shake hands with them,' said the other with a dry humour. 'Why does that interest you?'

'It just occurred to me that if they intended to destroy the station, then they would need something extremely powerful to do it.'

'A hydrogen bomb would finish us,' Brinson acknowledged, 'if it were dropped in the right place.'

'Even a small nuclear weapon could put you out of action for some time.'

'Well . . . yes, that is so,' agreed the other, reluctantly. 'But that's out of the question, of course. There are thousands, if not millions, of tons of solid ice on top of us and the tunnel leading down here has been strengthened tremendously. It may surprise you, but at high pressures and low enough temperatures such as can be got here, ice becomes as strong and unyielding as the best grades of steel. They could drop a dozen small atomic weapons up there without troubling us in the least. They could even block the tunnel if they were fantastically lucky in their aim, but that wouldn't put us out of action.'

'But just suppose that they were a little more clever than that,' suggested Carradine. 'Suppose that they did succeed in getting their hands on a nuclear weapon and brought it across the Red frontier which, as you say, is only a short distance away. It may then be possible for them to place that weapon here, inside the station, where they could do the maximum amount of damage, as well as kill most of the men from radioactive fallout in this confined space.'

Brinson's eyes measured Carradine slowly. 'You may have a point there,' he conceded. 'I must confess that the possibility had not occurred to me.'

'You can't be expected to think of everything,' Carradine said with a faint smile. 'It's pretty far-fetched. I just put it forward to indicate how vulnerable one can be without being aware of it.'

'Don't you think it strange, though, that our security people should have gone to all the trouble of importing you specially from England for this job?'

'Not really. If the agents of this organisation know most of your men by sight, it could be that a new face might get by. I seem to have done reasonably well so far.'

'I must admit that,' said Brinson a trifle grudgingly. 'You are to be given every facility while you are here unless it should endanger the station and the personnel.

I'll arrange for you to have living quarters here. At the moment, we are only about a quarter staffed, so we have plenty of room for an emergency such as this.'

'I'll be grateful for that.'

Brinson pressed a button on his desk. 'By the way,' he said, glancing up shrewdly. 'I suppose that until you find out something definite, every man, including me, will be a suspect?'

Carradine shrugged. 'I'm afraid so. All we know is that this organisation is the most powerful and dangerous that we have ever come across. The Russians have had us worried on several occasions in the past, but they've been child's play compared to these people. They seem to have had the ability to wait for an eternity for any act they wish to make. They've put their men into high places among the key positions of the Western world.' Carradine grinned. 'There have been times during the past few weeks when I've even had my doubts about the President.'

Carradine got to his feet as the other pushed back his chair and stood up. The door behind them opened and a man stepped into the office.

'Carstairs,' said Brinson quietly. 'I've arranged for Commander Carradine here to occupy Wellerby's quarters for the time being. Take him along, will you, and see that he's settled in all right.'

'Very good, sir.' Carstairs saluted, turned on his heel and stood on one side for Carradine to precede him. Outside in the corridor, he said with a warm, friendly smile: 'You seem to have merited the VIP treatment for some reason. You going to be staying here long, Commander?'

'I only wish I knew,' Carradine said easily. He found himself forming an instinctive liking for the other. 'I must say, though, that it's quite an experience being here. I never thought it possible that anything on this scale could be constructed out here. The work on it must have been tremendous.'

'It was.' The other led the way along two corridors and past several closed doors, finally pausing in front of one that bore the name *Captain Ronald C. Wellerby*. 'This is it,' he said. 'I hope you find it comfortable.'

'I'm sure I will. Where are the other men who usually work here?'

'Back in the States, most of them.' The other's cheerful face was sober. 'And, of course, we've lost some men in accidents.'

'You think they *were* accidents?'

'No one seems to know anything for sure. Maybe if we did it might remove a little of the uncertainty that seems to be hanging over the base.'

'I think I understand how it must feel.'

The other nodded, then said briskly: 'Dinner is at eight o'clock sharp. I understand you'll be dining with the Colonel. You'll doubtless meet most of the other officers then.'

★　★　★

There had been an unusual atmosphere at dinner that evening: sombre, dull and almost funereal. Carradine guessed that most of it stemmed from his presence there. These men at the station were not fools. Many of them had guessed by now why he was there, or had formed their own ideas.

Sitting on the edge of his bunk a little before midnight, Carradine ran over in his mind the names and faces of the men he had met during dinner. Lieutenant Venders had intrigued him particularly. Ever since that shot had been fired at him shortly after landing, he had wondered about this man. Those three men in the hut had stated that Venders had been there only a little while before, but had ostensibly returned to the base. He, though, Carradine reflected, had the best opportunity for being in a position to fire that shot. What Carradine had seen of him at dinner had heightened, rather than diminished, his suspicions. He was tall, well over six feet, and thin almost to the point of gauntness. His nose was long and aquiline, and his mouth seemed grotesquely small behind it; the thin, bristled moustache doing little to hide it. His eyes were dark, flecked with red, and brooding beneath the craggy, bushy brows that had a habit of drawing together into a straight line, wrinkling the brow above them. His manner seemed taciturn and saturnine. He spoke seldom, replying in terse monosyllables whenever a remark was addressed to him. Yet all the time, he seemed to be watching Carradine closely from beneath the lowered lids.

Carstairs was a different story. Forging a brilliant career at Yale before coming here, he had come out to station K with a reputation. He was, if anything, genius material. Here, he thought, was a man who made his own breaks as far as his career was concerned — an opportunist and a thinker, too, if his record was anything to go by.

Stretching himself out on the bunk, Carradine clasped his hands at the back of his neck and stared up thoughtfully at the ceiling. The air inside the small room was constantly warm and he could hear the faint sighing of the air conditioner somewhere out of sight. It was fantastic, this whole set-up, he thought inwardly — down here, a couple of hundred feet beneath the surface of the polar ice cap. Had he not seen that great, cavernous tunnel down which they had driven, he could not have imagined it. An entire city was here, hidden away from any prying eyes on the surface. Yet at any moment, it could be destroyed. Somewhere among the complement of the station was one man — perhaps more than one, and highly dangerous because they were not suspected — who was working for the Red Dragon. How long to discover which man it was?

The logical thing to do would be to begin snooping around the next day, trying not to make himself too obvious, but leaving no doubt in the minds of any enemies as to just why he was there. Sooner or later, there would be another attempt on his life. This time, he hoped he would be ready for it.

★　★　★

The next day, Carradine made a complete circuit of station K. Until then, he had not appreciated just how large the place was. There seemed to be everything there that a civilised community needed: shops, cinemas, workshops, places for relaxation, store rooms large enough to keep enough food to feed an army for several months. And here in the Arctic, there was little need for refrigeration. One merely arranged that no heating reached these rooms and any food kept virtually indefinitely.

On his way back to the main quarters, he met Venders. The other gave him a brief nod. 'Seen everything, Commander?' he asked. There was nothing friendly in his tone.

Carradine shrugged. 'Most of it,' he agreed. 'Naturally nobody will let me take a look at the heart of the place.'

'The atomic reactors, you mean?' There was a faint quirk around the corners of the other's mouth. 'If you really wish to see them — not that there's much you can actually see — I'll take you down.'

'Why — thanks.' Carradine fell into step beside the other. In his pocket, the comforting weight of the Luger rested snugly against his body. He kept his right hand there.

Venders led the way down one of the shallowly sloping corridors cut into the ice. At the far end there was an elevator in which they plummeted down into the very bowels of the ice cap. Carradine felt his stomach rise up with a swift rush, and watched Venders out of the corner of his vision as the other thumbed the buttons near the iron-grille door.

The door slid back as the elevator came to a halt. Venders motioned him forward. 'Here we are,' he said quietly. 'This is what makes this station possible. Without it, we'd probably all be frozen to death in a very short time.'

'Would it be easy to sabotage the reactors?' Carradine asked directly.

'If you mean could someone destroy them, I suppose that it is possible. But they would have to know plenty about them. No use putting a few sticks of dynamite in here and hoping to do it that way.'

'Then how would they do it?'

'Are you serious?' The other took his arm and led him forward. The pulsing note of the giant turbines that virtually ran station K was a purring, sing-song note in his ears and the whole place seemed to be alive with shuddering, invisible energies.

A few moments later, he came to an

abrupt halt. There was a low handrail in front of him and he found himself looking down into what seemed to be a vast amphitheatre. Down below them, some eighty or ninety feet away he guessed, were banks of instruments stretched around the wide floor in a great semi-circle. There were five men working below. None of them looked up as Carradine looked down at them.

'You haven't answered my question,' Carradine said quietly. 'How could anyone sabotage this?' He waved a hand to indicate the tremendous sweep of the instrument panels with the thousands of lights flashing on and off along the tiered banks.

'The reactors are controlled mainly by rods of some neutron-absorbing material, heavy water or boron. They are pushed in or pulled out to control the rate of the nuclear reaction. All one would have to do would be to override the automatic controls and keep the rods out. That way, the reaction would become critical in a reasonably short space of time.'

'How long?' Carradine persisted.

207

Venders pursed his lips. 'Hard to say with any real degree of accuracy. A few hours maybe. Certainly not much longer.'

'And then there would be one almighty bang and everything would be disintegrated.'

'Exactly.' The other moved along the circular platform, pausing and pointing directly beneath him. 'There is the main control panel. You can just see it if you lean over the rail.'

Carradine moved up beside him, gripped the rail tightly and leaned forward. Directly below him, he could make out the edge of the control panel, a row of brilliant green lights stretching across its face. Then, without warning, there was a sharp, rending crash that came from somewhere very close at hand and he felt himself being thrust forward into empty space as the metal rail snapped under his weight, pitching him away from the platform.

For a long drawn-out second, it seemed inevitable that he should plunge all the way down to the floor of the control room below. Then something caught at his back. For a moment he hung there, feet scrabbling for a hold on the platform. His arms flailed desperately and then, miraculously, he was back on his feet, all the breath gone from his lungs, a pounding in his ears as the blood rushed through his temples.

Slowly, as he edged his way back from the platform rim, Venders released his tight-fisted grip on him.

'You all right?' There was no doubting the note of concern in his tone. It could have been simulated, of course, Carradine thought quickly. He was back on balance now. Yet if the other had tried to kill him, why had he saved his life at the very last second? It didn't make sense. Certainly the man he was looking for would never have a lapse of conscience like that. Rubbing the back of his hand over his perspiring forehead, he moved cautiously towards the broken rail.

'Funny that it should have snapped like that,' said Venders, going down carefully on one knee. Down below, the technicians were staring up at them in stunned surprise.

Carefully, Carradine ran his fingers along the broken edge of the metal. At last, he gave a nod of brief satisfaction. 'Quite simple,' he said gently. 'It's been sawn through here so that any weight against it would cause it to break.'

Venders' eyes widened a little. 'Then it was another try at murder.'

8

Flight Into Danger

It was on the next day that Carradine asked to have a further talk with Colonel Brinson. He had briefly mentioned the incident in the reactor room, but had asked the other to say nothing about it to any of the other men.

'I've been giving this *accident* a great deal of thought since we last met,' Brinson said as he waved the other to a chair. 'I suppose that until this happened I had been fooling myself all along the line that there was little to these events beyond coincidence. Whenever you get men cooped up here for months on end, there are bound to be side-effects, tempers become frayed, nerves stretched taut, and men are bound to make errors of judgement which can look worse than they really are.'

'But now that you're quite convinced?'

Brinson gave a helpless movement of his left hand. 'I have to be,' he admitted. 'Here we have the most secret base the United States possesses, yet clearly the enemy knows of its existence — must have known for a long time if you're right about them — and not only that, but somehow they have succeeded in placing at least one of their top men here, right under our very noses. And all the time, we felt sure that our security was sufficient to rule out any possibility of this ever happening.'

'I'm afraid that we all seem to have underestimated these people to the danger point. God knows how many there are, and what sort of devilry they're up to at this very moment.'

'What do you want me to do in this matter?' Brinson spread his hands flat on top of the desk. 'As you have made absolutely clear, I can trust no one here. I'm even beginning to suspect myself.'

'I've virtually ruled out Lieutenant Venders,' Carradine said quietly. 'I must confess that he was my first suspect. He was apparently with the men in the surface huts and could have fired that shot at me. His manner was certainly not calculated to diminish my suspicious. Yet on the other hand, he would not have saved me from that fall unless he was innocent.'

'He could have done that with the idea of diverting suspicion from himself, especially if he got it into his head that you were on to him.'

'True. But I've no doubt in my mind that an eighty-foot drop would have been more than enough to kill me. Even a cat wouldn't have landed on his feet after that drop. So Venders must have known such a fall would have had fatal consequences. Yet he pulled me back and at considerable risk to himself. I'm no lightweight, as you can guess.'

'So where do you go from here?'

'I'd like your cooperation in a little scheme I have in mind to smoke our friend out into the open.' Carradine leaned forward conspiratorially. 'He's jumpy now — nervous. He can feel the net beginning to close in on him and like most men in his position, he knows the

213

consequences of failure. I'm certain that he'll make his move in the very near future.'

*   *   *

Carradine took one comprehensive look around and then pulled his body back out of sight behind the tall console. He leaned against the cool metal and waited, the smooth solidity of the Luger cradled in his holster. There was no sound in the vast control room beyond the endless, eternal pulsing of the mighty engines that pumped electrical energy and warmth around the entire confines of Station K. Without the beating of this massive heart, flooding the arteries with light and heat, the station would die. Worse than that, if the reaction inside the atomic reactors got out of control, everything would go up in one hellish flare of radiation. The seismographs all over the world would record a tremor close to the North Pole and then, slowly, the full report would come in of an atomic explosion on the ice pack. There would, however, be nobody left here to be aware of this.

He tried to find himself a more comfortable position. Outside, it would be night now. A bitter night full of the freezing wind, the lancing shards of ice and the brilliant light of stars and aurora which made up the polar night. Down here, everything was on automatic. No one attended the reactors. If anything went wrong, machines put it right or gave audible warning in sufficient time for technicians to arrive and rectify matters.

Carradine glanced down at his watch. Ten-thirty. Would the Red Dragon agent make his move tonight? It seemed probable. Brinson had done everything Carradine had asked. There would be an unusually long gap between the changing of the men on watch. During that time, a man could get down into the control room, set the control rods and leave, making his way over to the Russian border to the east before the nuclear bomb exploded.

The minutes ticked by very slowly. The pulsing hum went on and on, forming a background noise which gradually became unnoticed except when he concentrated

215

on it. Eleven o'clock. Still no sound that would indicate the presence of another human being nearby.

Had he been mistaken? Had the other been too clever for him, seen through the trap, and was determined to ignore it — to get Carradine on his own terms at a time and place of his own choosing? Gently, he eased himself forward and peered cautiously around the edge of the huge console. Only the flickering rows of green lights gave any light to the control room. They seemed to flash through the entire spectrum of colour as he watched. No doubt the men who attended the gigantic machines, and who controlled this terrible power, knew what each light meant; but to him it appeared simply as a maze of colour that was oddly straining on the vision. He shut his eyes to squeeze out the glare, then opened them again swiftly and instinctively as a faint half-heard whisper of sound reached him. The fact that he had picked it out above the much louder, more insistent throb of the turbines meant one thing: that it had to be an extraneous sound, immediately making itself heard.

For several seconds afterwards, there was nothing. He strained his eyes and ears to pick out something that would give him a lead. At first — nothing. Then something moved, slowly and cautiously on the very edge of his vision: a humped shadow making its way down the flight of stairs from the circular platform overlooking the wide spread of the floor.

He tried to make out who the other was. Not tall enough to be either Venders or Brinson. Theoretically, it could have been anyone on the station, he told himself. He waited tensely as the other came forward. The gun felt heavy in his right hand. Acting on impulse, he thrust it back into his pocket. Now that he knew where the other was, he felt he had no immediate need of the weapon. He wanted to take this man alive if he could. Maybe, thought Carradine — though it was extremely doubtful — he could get the other to talk once he realised that he had failed in his mission.

Less than twelve feet from where Carradine crouched stood the control panel which Venders had pointed out to him; the one which controlled the reactor rods that held everything in equilibrium. He guessed that this man would pull the control rods and then try to make a break for it. Somehow, Carradine had to stop him before he succeeded. Deliberately, he tensed himself and braced his legs beneath him, ready to hurl himself forward across the intervening distance. The man padded forward on soft feet, making scarcely any sound. His face was still an anonymous black shadow in which Carradine could make out nothing to give him a clue as to the other's identity. Then, slipping forward, the other moved over to the control panel and the greenish glow from the lights fell full on his face.

Carradine sucked in a breath. It was Lieutenant Carstairs. Narrowing his eyes, he waited until the other had paused in front of the panel. He saw the man's right hand to go out towards the controls, then made his move.

Some hidden instinct warned Carstairs of his danger. Carradine had covered half the distance when the other turned, spinning abruptly on his heel. His hand dropped towards his belt and the lips were drawn back into a savage snarl that completely altered his features. Now there seemed something diabolical about the greenish face that stared out at Carradine.

There was a faint glint of light on metal as the other tugged at the gun in his pocket. It would be a near thing, Carradine thought. He struck downward with the flat edge of his right hand. The other moved back a pace and the blow merely caught him lightly on the wrist, but it was sufficient to deflect the weapon. Carstairs squeezed the trigger instinctively and there was a shrill, high-pitched whine as the slug ricocheted off the hard floor and smashed into the face of the console on the opposite side of the room. Carradine's muscles coiled as he struck again, aiming for the exposed throat. Carstairs uttered a wailing cry and fell back against the panel. His scrambling fingers caught at the control. With a sudden movement, he jerked, and in the same instant a row of lights above the panel flickered amber, then began to switch to red one by one.

'Damn you,' he muttered through twisted lips. 'That's the control rods out. Another fifteen minutes and all of this goes up.'

Desperately, Carradine tried to move forward. Carstairs effectively blocked his way. A bunched fist caught Carradine on the side of his head, knocking him sideways off balance; and in the same moment, the other flung himself forward, dropping all of his weight on Carradine's prone body. Carradine's teeth ground together in his mouth as all of the air in his lungs gushed out through his lips. He felt the other scrambling for his throat, felt the taloned hands get their grip on his neck, beginning to squeeze inexorably.

His body was being twisted and thrust down. Nails dug deeply into the flesh of his throat. The pounding roar of the whining turbines became overlaid by another thudding sound: the beat of his own bottled-up blood as it tried to get down into his body, and the tortured rasp of air whistling in and out of his constricted throat.

Half on his back, he kicked out blindly with his left foot. The toecap of his shoe hit something soft and yielding and there came a momentary scream of pain from the man on top of him. For a second, the tortuous pressure on his throat eased and he gulped air down into his heaving lungs. He hammered out again with his leg, but the other had shifted his position slightly and he found that it made no difference now what he did. Over the other's lowered head he saw that all of the lights on the console were now glaring redly in the multi-coloured dimness. The twisted, grimacing face drew closer as Carstairs leaned all of his weight forward in one last effort.

Then, abruptly, the pale reds and greens vanished, wiped out in the harsh, actinic glare of white light. Carstairs jerked up his head and stared behind him. Dimly, Carradine was aware of shouts in the distance, of footsteps clattering on the metal stairs. Sweat ran into his eyes, stinging and half-blinding them as he acted instinctively. Exerting all of the strength left in him, he jerked his arms wide, freeing them from the other's weight. Gasping air down into his body, focusing his gaze on the other, he swung both hands straight and stiff into the other's body, down near the soft parts in the middle.

Carstairs uttered a harsh, bleating gasp of agony. Thrusting upwards with his knees, Carradine managed to hurl him away. Carstairs fell over onto his side and lay there for a moment, then heaved himself onto his feet and ran for the dim shadows that lay beneath the overhanging platform.

The first men reached the floor, then started after him. Straightening up onto his hands and knees, Carradine yelled in a harsh croak: 'Watch him! He's got a gun and he'll use it.'

'You're damned right he will,' Carstairs yelled back. 'And don't forget that those bars are out. Only a little longer and everything goes up.'

The other punctuated his yell with a couple of shots. One of the men at the bottom of the stairs went down as his kneecap was smashed by the bullet. Another slumped sideways. Then the men were closing in from all sides. With an effort, Carradine thrust himself to his feet. His body felt numbed and bruised in every limb and each breath he took burned in his throat.

Venders came hurrying forward and Brinson was close on his heels.

With a jerk of his shoulders, Carradine pointed to the control panel nearby. 'You'd better check that,' he said, forcing the words out from swollen lips. 'He's pulled out the control rods.'

Brinson took everything in at once. Good man, thought Carradine as the other turned and began giving orders. He didn't waste time asking questions. He got going right away.

'You'd better sit down,' said Venders. 'No need to worry now. Everything is under control.'

'But Carstairs . . . ' Carradine struggled to push the other's restraining hands away but Venders held him down and shook his head.

'Carstairs — or whatever his real name is — won't be giving us any further trouble.'

Carradine lifted his head. Very slowly, it

dawned on him that there was very little noise in the room beyond the humming lilt of the dynamos. He stared beyond Venders, into the dark shadows beneath the platform. Almost directly under the spot where he had almost fallen to his death, something humped and dark lay silent on the floor, arms and legs outstretched. He nodded his head very slowly in understanding.

Brinson came over and stood, looking down at him for a long moment before speaking, then said: 'There wasn't enough time for him to do any real, permanent damage. The reactors will be functioning normally again in ten minutes or so.'

Carradine shook his head in an effort to clear it of the fog that swirled around in his brain. There was something in the back of his mind that desperately needed to come out into the open where he could recognise it. He lurched to his feet and stared at Brinson. 'Where do you keep the transmitter?' he asked throatily.

'Why on the surface, of course. What's on your mind?'

'It's just possible that Carstairs had an

accomplice. It isn't usual for these men to work as lone wolves whenever there's something as vitally important as this at stake. If he has, then my guess is that he's waiting near the transmitter, ready to send off a message saying whether their attempt has been successful or a failure.'

'Carstairs may have intended doing that himself,' suggested Venders.

'Perhaps. But it's a chance we can't afford to take. I suggest that the sooner we get to the transmitter, the better.'

$$\star \quad \star \quad \star$$

Muffled up in the thick furs — for he had insisted on accompanying the party — Carradine stared out into the deep velvet blackness of the Arctic night. A million stars seemed to glitter brilliantly in those stygian depths and beneath them, the snow took up the pale light, reflected it and threw it back into the sky and into the eyes of the men who emerged one by one out of the tunnel into the open. The wind had died

225

completely. Everywhere, there was a deep silence that went beyond anything that Carradine had ever experienced before. It stretched clear from one distant horizon to another, pressing down on them with an intensity that could be felt.

Venders moved up beside him and peered at him from behind the goggles he wore. His face was a pale grey blur under the thick furry hood. He pointed a gloved finger towards the huts in the distance, placed his head close to Carradine's and said loudly: 'Take a look. See the light there?'

Carradine nodded. There was indeed a light, standing out starkly against the blackness on all sides. There was only a pale glow, gleaming through a small square window in one of the huts, and in the daylight it would have been lost; but in this all-pervading darkness, it stood out clearly.

'That's the transmitter room,' Venders said. 'Looks as though you were right after all. He's got a pal in there.'

'Probably waiting for him to arrive with news,' Carradine said tensely. 'My bet is that the transmitting channel is open; that he's in constant touch with his home base — wherever that may be.'

Venders nodded, then motioned to the small party of determined men, all armed with automatic rifles. Brinson was taking no chances on this man getting away, Carradine thought grimly.

They made their way over the smooth snow. It would have been easier to take one of the snowcats; but in this silence, the sound of the powerful engines would have been heard for miles. Had there been a blizzard blowing they would have taken that chance, for the howling, shrieking wind would have drowned out any lesser sound. The ice sloped up sharply to the plateau on which the huts were situated. Reaching a spot twenty yards from that which showed the light, Venders motioned his men to take up their positions so that the hut was completely surrounded. Carradine watched the way in which the men moved with a singleness of design that indicated that they must have done this sort of thing before. When they were in place, not a mouse could have got out of the hut without being seen.

Hefting his rifle into his right hand, Venders moved towards the closed door. A faint crack of light showed just beneath it. Carradine followed close on the other's heels. He had no idea how many men there might be in there — one or half a dozen — each willing to sell their life dearly; knowing that if they failed, their fate would be far worse than a quick death from a bullet.

Venders paused outside the door, motioned Carradine over to the other side to cover him, then lifted his foot and kicked the door in with a savage thrust of his boot. It crashed back on splintered hinges. Slightly off balance, Venders half-fell into the room, jerking up the barrel of the rifle as he did so.

The man seated behind the transmitter whirled swiftly. There was the glint of light on the automatic which appeared as if by magic in his right hand. Carradine held his breath as he fired instinctively, the Luger jerking against his wrist. The man uttered a sharp cry as the heavy weapon went flying from his smashed fingers, ending up in the corner of the room.

Venders moved forward and yanked the other man to his feet. 'Carlsen,' he said dully. 'So you're in this dirty business. One of the last men I would have expected.'

'You know nothing,' snarled the other through lips thinned back over his teeth. He cradled his bloodied hand against his stomach, holding it with the other.

'We know enough,' Carradine said tautly. 'Your friend Carstairs, or whatever his name was, is no longer with us. He made his play — and failed. Just as you have.'

The other said nothing, staring sullenly at the men gathered about him.

Carradine said very softly: 'I don't suppose you'll talk willingly. Your kind don't. But we have ways of getting the truth out of you.'

'You'll get nothing from me,' said the other viciously.

'We'll see.'

Three hours later, with a couple of straight bourbons inside him, Carradine sat back in the chair in Brinson's office, feeling more relaxed than at any time since he arrived there. And yet there was something curiously wrong about everything. He was unable to put his finger on it, but it was nevertheless nagging at him relentlessly.

'You look like a man who has something on his mind, rather than one who should be feeling extremely pleased with himself,' observed Brinson, leaning forward and pouring more bourbon into the other's glass.

'Just a feeling,' Carradine said, jerking his mind back to the present.

'You think we didn't get them all?' For a moment, there was a note of apprehension in Brinson's tone.

'I think we got all the men at the station,' Carradine said with conviction. 'But it seems to me that both Carstairs and his accomplice had been forewarned about me, yet my coming here supposed to be top secret.'

'The men at the Alaska airbase knew,' Brinson pointed out.

'I don't think that's the answer. This operation must have taken these two some time to arrange. If it had been someone at the airbase, they would have had about twenty-four hours at the most. I doubt if that would have been long enough.'

'So it must have been someone in New York or Washington.'

'Exactly.' Carradine got to his feet. 'With your permission, I'd like to have another go at the prisoner. The sooner I get him to talk, the easier I shall feel in my mind.'

'You don't have to have my permission for that, Commander,' said the other quietly. 'Go ahead with whatever you have to do. If you need any help, just let me know.'

★ ★ ★

The cab drew up outside the tall building in New York. Carradine got out, stretched his legs, glanced down at his watch, then paid the driver. He stood for a moment savouring the cool air on the street, staring up at the great concrete and glass erection that stretched up to where the woolly white clouds paced slowly across the deep blue sky. It was a beautiful day for so late in the autumn.

He felt tense inwardly, but showed none of it outwardly. The Luger nestled warmly against his ribs as he ran up the stairs and into the wide entrance. He knew his way now along the various corridors and up in the sighing elevators. Five minutes after entering the building, he was standing just outside the glass-panelled door of Dean's office. He rapped sharply with his knuckles. There was a momentary pause, then he heard the command to enter.

Dean was seated behind the desk as Carradine remembered him. The other gave him a faint look of surprise, then waved a hand to the chair. 'I didn't expect to see you back for another two or three days,' he said genially. 'Naturally, I got the preliminary report from Station K. You did a very fine piece of work there.'

'There were one or two moments when I didn't feel too sure of myself,' Carradine said, forcing himself to relax.

Dean raised his bushy brows for a moment. 'You surprise me,' he said softly, but with a new note in his tone. 'I thought you were the completely self-reliant agent.'

'That is often the case,' Carradine said, nodding his head a little. 'But there have been sufficient times in the past when the cards have been stacked against me from the very beginning, for me to be able to recognise a set-up when I find myself right in the middle of it.'

Dean pursed his lips and pushed his chair a little closer to the desk. 'I'm not sure that I follow you,' he said harshly.

'Someone took the trouble to warn not only the enemy cell working in Socorro all about me, but those Red Dragon agents in Station K.'

'Can you be sure of this?'

'I think so.' Carradine could feel a faint sheen of perspiration on his forehead, but he tried not to think of the possible consequences if he was wrong. Now he would have to play the hand he had been dealt by fate all the way through to the bitter end.

Dean nodded his head. 'You returned here after arriving back from Alaska?'

'Not directly. I called at Washington on my way here. One or two points I had to verify.'

Dean's eyes seemed to narrow just a fraction. 'I'm still a little in the dark. Perhaps you can enlighten me.'

'It's quite simple, really,' Carradine said. 'I'm not sure when I first suspected that every move I made had been given to the Red Dragon in advance. It was in Socorro, I think. I went along to see Cornish and decided to put the fear of God into him, force his hand, make him act rashly, thinking that he was already a suspect — that events were closing in on him.'

'And it worked perfectly,' put in the other.

'Not exactly. They made their play before I was ready. It was almost the end for Steve Carradine. Had I not been fantastically lucky, I would have been dead by now or in the same position as that poor devil who was dragged out of the alley in the Bronx. But as I was saying, they knew all about me; were even expecting me. It might have been a coincidence, of course. This mission seems to have been plagued with what seemed like coincidences on the surface. But it wasn't. They knew all about me. And at Station K, the position was just the same. They were waiting for me — first with a high-powered rifle, and then with part of the handrail in the reactor room sawn through. Everything could be made to look like an accident.'

'And you are now suggesting that one of my men here in New York is in league with the Red Dragon — that he deliberately betrayed you to them?'

'No.' Very slowly, Carradine shook his head. 'I'm prepared to go even further than that. I know who did it. Perhaps the top agent they have in this country. The man the CIA have been looking for these past five years; the man they'd give their eye teeth to lay by the heels.'

'May I ask who he is?'

Sitting forward a little, giving the impression that he was completely relaxed, Carradine smiled. His muscles were tautly tensed, however, and he sat waiting for any movement on the other's part; any trick. 'Really, it's no use trying to bluff it out any longer. I know that you are playing a double game: working for the Red Dragon, occupying this important position of trust where you can be of the most of value to them.'

Dean's face had not changed. There was a tiny muscle twitching in his cheek, but that was all that betrayed the emotions in his mind at that moment. Then, in a very quiet and polite voice, he said: 'I'm afraid that these events must have proved too much for you. You have been overtaxed and overworked. Perhaps if I were to have a word on the transatlantic telephone with your superiors, they might send you on vacation for — '

'You never give up, do you?' Carradine smiled broadly. 'Carstairs was, unfortunately, killed before he could talk, but that other agent was able to give me quite a lot of important information. It included your name. Of course, he had to be persuaded to talk, but we have our own methods, just as you have yours.'

'You're lying,' said Dean. 'Besides, one word from me would mean the end of you. No one will believe this wild story of yours. Do you seriously think they will?'

'Oh, I'm quite sure they will.' Carradine took the heavy Luger from his pocket, the barrel pointed at Dean's chest. 'And perhaps I ought to point out that at this distance, it will be quite impossible for me to miss, especially such a target as yourself.'

The other hissed something in what Carradine took to be Chinese. Certainly it did not seem to be Russian or any other language that he had ever heard spoken.

'And what do you expect to do now?' asked the other after a long silence. 'You may find it difficult to walk out of here, taking me at gunpoint. There are several of my men in the building. Perhaps they are not Red Dragon agents — for the most part they are fools — but one word from me would be believed.'

'I've already considered that.' Carradine sat back, regarding the other evenly. 'We'll just sit here for a little while. If anyone comes to you, then it will be just too bad.'

'On the contrary,' said a voice Carradine remembered from a short time before.

'You will be the one to walk out of here — and very soon.'

Minden came into the room from one of the smaller offices. There was a snub-nosed automatic in his right hand and it was trained directly on Carradine. 'I suggest that you relinquish your hold on that gun, otherwise I shall be forced to use this now. As you may know, it will make very little sound.'

Reluctantly, Carradine dropped the Luger onto the floor at his feet. There was a broad smile of triumph on Dean's fleshy features. 'The tables are turned, are they not, my impetuous friend?'

'You must have been at this game for a long time,' Carradine said grudgingly. 'You're too good to have just joined the ranks of these men.'

'Fifteen years.' There was a touch of pride in the other's voice. 'It may be that our usefulness here is finished now. But somehow, I feel that we shall receive a warm welcome when we return home.'

'And you think that you'll get out of the country?' Carradine asked. 'Surely you don't think I would be fool enough to keep this information to myself.'

Dean shrugged. 'It is really quite immaterial to us whether you have or not. You people are fools. You underestimate us to the extent that you believe yourselves to be the Lords of creation. That is your greatest mistake. When will you learn that our organisation is far better than yours? Our escape route has been in existence for several years, waiting for the moment when we should have to use it.' He shook his head. 'No, my friend. You will be dead and we will be on our way and none of your CIA agents will be any the wiser.' Heaving back his chair, he pushed himself to his feet and glanced across at Minden. 'You know what to do with our friend,' he said. 'Be sure that there is no mistake this time.'

Carrodine got slowly to his feet as Minden advanced on him. He said quite slowly and deliberately: 'I warned you both.' He looked down at the watch on his wrist and twisted the knob slightly, almost unconsciously. 'Evidently you've forgotten, Dean, that I called at Washington on my way here. I didn't do that for the sake of my health, you know. I warned the CIA of what I know. My guess is that they will be knocking on this door in precisely ten seconds from now.'

Minden paused less than a foot away, the gun still trained on Carradine. He looked uncertainly at Dean.

'Can't you see that he's lying, that he's just trying to play for time?' snapped the other thickly. 'Take him out and — '

There came a sharp knock on the door.

Dean stared at it. Minden looked too, and in that second Carradine's arm moved. It moved only a few inches, and Minden gave a yelp as the glass face of the watch struck him on the back of the hand. Savagely, grunting something unintelligible under his breath, he swung back. His fingers tightened on the trigger of the automatic. Then his eyes rolled up until only the whites showed and he collapsed at Carradine's feet as though pole-axed.

Behind the desk, Dean lunged forward, scrabbling for one of the drawers. He had it open less than three inches when the side of Carradine stiffened hand hit him just behind the left ear and he continued to fall forward until his head hit hard on the edge of the mahogany desk.

Almost casually, Carradine walked over to the door and opened it. 'They're all yours,' he said, pointing to the two unconscious bodies in the room.

* ★ *

When Minden had been taken away and the questioning was over, Carradine made his way down in the gently sighing elevator, through the entrance, and stepped out onto the sidewalk. The sky was still a deep blue, but there was a faint chill in the air and the few clouds he could see in the west were orange-tipped spears. Pulling up the collar of his coat, he began walking slowly along the sidewalk away from the building.

He scarcely noticed the white car that glided smoothly along the street and followed him for a few moments before stopping near the kerb. Turning his head, he glanced at it curiously and made to move on, then stopped as if thunderstruck.

'Candy!' He walked quickly over to the

241

car. 'How on earth did you get here?'

'Does it matter?' she asked lightly. 'I saw them take those two men away a little while ago. Is that the case closed as far as you are concerned?'

'I guess so.' He nodded.

'Then it will be back to London and out of my life, I suppose.'

'I'm afraid so.' He tried to read what was going on in her mind from the expression in her eyes.

'How long do you have in New York?'

'Two, three days perhaps. I'll send off my report tomorrow.'

'We could see a lot of New York in three days,' she said, and there was something more serious in her tone. She opened the car door. Carradine hesitated for only a second, then slid in beside her. The engine purred softly as they moved away from the sidewalk and into the stream of early evening traffic.

THE END